# Nine Simple Patterns for Complicated Women

# Nine Simple Patterns for Complicated Women

*stories*

## Mary Rechner

Published by Propeller Books, Portland, Oregon.
ISBN 978-0-9827704-0-5
First U.S. Edition 2010

Cover concept by Dan DeWeese
Cover art by Matt Hall
Cover design by Benjamin Craig

Stories from this book originally appeared in the following: "Teeth" in *Kenyon Review*; "Special Ability" in *Washington Square*; "Exhibit" in *Propeller*, "Pattern" on *Kenyon Review Online*, "Four" on *Literary Mama*; "Moon" on *Oregon Literary Review*; and "Hot Springs" in a saddle-stitched letterpress edition by Cloverfield Press.

www.propellerbooks.com

Printed in Canada

For Barry

# CONTENTS

# PATTERN

SILVIA HOPED her scissors were sharp enough. The triplets were finally asleep and John was next door, playing poker. The old sewing machine, dusted, sat on the kitchen table. The ironing board stood next to the sink, and on it waited the iron, filled with water for steam and plugged in, though not yet turned on. All she needed was a trio of happy seamstresses: one to cut the fabric, one to stitch it, one to press the seams. But she wasn't Cinderella. It amazed her, how the triplets loved those grisly fairytales. She tried in vain to get them to understand the sexist subtexts. "Keep reading," the girls insisted. "Just read."

The phone rang. "Tell me when your anniversary is again?" Annie's voice. Half shaky, half sly.

"Tomorrow."

"And you're making a dress tonight?"

"I haven't even started!"

"I guess I'll watch the guys play poker," Annie said. On poker night Silvia and Annie always held party night. They toyed with inviting other women, but never followed through. Other women would complicate the routine. Silvia drank white wine. Annie liked hard lemonade. The radio D.J. played songs from the eighties and they danced in the living room without turning on the lights.

"Send John some good vibes so we can pay the baby-sitter tomorrow!" Silvia said, trying to end the conversation on a note of gaiety, but Annie hung up before she could get to the exclamation point. Silvia could tell Annie was pissed. Annie loved party night, loved getting out her hoop earrings, red lipstick, and an old Echo and the Bunnymen t-shirt, the neck cut wide so it slid off her shoulder.

Tomorrow morning Silvia's triplets would traipse over to Annie's house, still in their footie pajamas, to watch cartoons with Annie's twins. When Silvia reclaimed her daughters at noon, Annie would probably still be angry, her grim smile almost impossible to dislodge.

It was time for a drink. The white wine was easy to locate in the refrigerator, but the corkscrew required a search through the junk drawer. Why Silvia wanted to sew a dress when she could go to a store and buy one much more easily, even more cheaply, she didn't know. She felt like making something that didn't get eaten, felt like doing something that didn't get undone almost immediately: cooking, dishes, laundry, vacuuming. She leaned back against the sink and imagined her husband John next door in Annie's kitchen, playing poker with Annie's husband Saul and the other neighborhood dads. Annie probably wasn't even watching them play. She was probably perched on a stool in the second floor bathroom, smoking out the window and picking at her cuticles.

The back of Silvia's shirt was damp where she leaned against the sink. Intense mothering. These two words jumped in her head, the wine slowing the bounce just a little. In fact, this period of intense mothering was drawing to a close. The girls were growing up. Like a flood or tornado, it was easier to conceptualize early childhood as it wound down. In the midst of it there had been too many diapers, tantrums, breast infections, jars of baby food, rashes, bloody lips, chest colds, financial crises, bumped heads, swollen gums, months without sex, nights without sleep, and days off from preschool to reflect with any depth. This year the triplets finally started full-day kindergarten. John's vasectomy was long healed. Time to figure out what next.

Silvia poured another glass of wine. In a minute she would definitely begin to sew, but first she pictured herself sauntering into the restaurant in her new black dress.

"I'll have the *steak au poivre*," she'd say, confident of both her pronunciation and that *poivre* meant pepper.

"You're amazing," John would say.

In real life John was much more suspicious. In real life he'd hiss, *What's with the French?*

In a moment she would spread the black linen out across the kitchen table so she could trace the pattern with chalk and cut it.

The phone rang again.

"John just won a hand," reported Annie. "Saul's won two. Have you seen Marty, Barbara's husband, lately? I swear he weighs fifty pounds more than last month."

"Where are you?" Silvia asked. Annie sounded strange.

"In the hall closet. How's the dress?"

"Don't ask. Why are you in the closet?"

"Have you ever felt like you were being swallowed?"

"What do you mean?" Silvia asked. But she knew what Annie meant. Annie's twins were three years old and never slept at the same time. On party/poker night Annie gave them each a spoonful of Robitussin P.M.

"I mean suffocated. Or choked. Or trapped. I can't tell." Annie was crying, her voice raspy and loud.

"Did you take your meds today?" Silvia finished the rest of her wine and poured another glass. After two glasses she felt her body, gravity, the kitchen tiles under her bare feet. Usually her head was in charge.

"Yes, I took my meds." Annie sounded sullen, adolescent.

"You have to quit smoking."

"I know."

"Come over." Silvia hung up the phone. She knew Annie was already opening the gate between their two backyards, but she tilted the pattern and material out of its paper bag and slid it onto the table. The pencil-drawn woman on the front of the packet had no face, but she looked good anyway, legs apart, hip thrust forward. Her heels were extremely high. *Make it Tonight, Wear it Tomorrow!* exclaimed the envelope. The dress was a halter that tied around the neck. At this moment it looked a little like the dresses Wilma and Betty wore on *The Flintstones.*

Annie was waving at the kitchen door. Silvia let her in.

"How's the dress. Are you almost finished?" Annie put her bottles of lemonade in the refrigerator and tossed a package of salami onto the counter.

"You've got to stop asking me that! I've barely started."

"Okay!" Annie turned the radio up and started poking through the cabinets. She wasn't crying anymore.

"Top shelf," Silvia reminded her, but Annie had already

found the ashtray. She perched on the countertop, slid the window above the sink open, and lit her cigarette.

"Much better," she said, exhaling through the screen and shutting her eyes.

Silvia unfolded the black linen, smoothing it flat with her hand and placing the thin brown paper pattern on top of the fabric. Perhaps all Annie needed was a moment of repose, a few bottles of hard lemonade, and a cigarette. The other mothers Silvia knew might go out and have a glass of wine, but it was one or maybe two glasses, period. They definitely didn't smoke. Their opinions about fluoride in the water and college funds and when their daughters could get their ears pierced were all firmly in place. On the one hand, this certainty was enviable. On the other, it was incredibly boring.

"I'm thinking about going back to work," Silvia said, pulling a pin from the tomato pin cushion.

"That's interesting." This was Annie's standard initial response. It wasn't irritating. It was good. Annie was a thinker. She didn't act like she knew it all already. She didn't run home and Google answers. She liked to really talk things through. The problem was, there wasn't always enough time to talk, and when she was really depressed she didn't want to. (When she was really depressed, her voice rose in a plaintive whine: "Why do we have to worry about everything so much? These details about other people's lives are rotting my brain." Silvia found that thinking about her children as "other people" actually helped relieve the pressure a bit.)

Before Silvia pinned the pattern to the fabric there was another step, but she couldn't remember what it was.

"Maybe our girls would be happier without mothers," Annie said. The ash on her cigarette was long. Her eyes were wide and bright with anxiety. "If you go back to work, who will I hang out with?" She set her cigarette in the ashtray and began rolling a slice of salami.

"You have other friends. Plus the kids."

"I'm not even going to comment on your first sentence." Annie took a bite of salami. "And I like the kids best these days when they're both asleep."

"I like the girls best when they're eating without complaining." Silvia remembered the step she forgot. She couldn't just pin the pattern to the fabric—first she had to cut the pattern out. "I like watching them chewing and getting full."

"I like that, too." Annie pushed the rest of the tube of salami into her mouth.

"I haven't sewn a dress since high school," Silvia said. "I need to concentrate." She was feeling a bit panicked, and that was unnecessary. She needed to read the instructions. It would all come back: bias, seam allowance, basting, darts. She had chosen an easy pattern, a dress without a zipper, on purpose.

"Just relax. You'll figure it out. I'm going to lie down on the kitchen floor just because I want to, okay?" Annie hopped off the counter and stretched out on her back next to the ironing board.

Silvia made sure not to step on her. She had to watch what she said to Annie. A while back she made the mistake of wondering about the "spirit world" during a conversation, and it had launched a chain reaction: candles, chanting, crystals, chakras, and channeling. Annie found them a shaman. For five hundred dollars, the shaman cleansed their souls with a small drum and some incense in a dim room over a pizza parlor, and Silvia felt good for a few weeks, really good, as if the litany of her life's imperfections—monotonous mothering, clueless husband, ten extra pounds—was now merely humorous. The problem was that this advanced wisdom didn't stick, but instead drained like a dying battery. No, not like a battery. It felt hacked into like a stick of butter, until she was as sloppy and unformed as the melting mess on the dish next to the toaster.

Silvia took a deep breath and began to cut the pieces of the pattern. Her scissors were duller than sewing scissors should be, but these were not the ones the triplets had used to cut telephone wire, so at least these cut. How had she forgotten that in high school she had relied heavily on the Home Ec teacher's expertise? Ms. Armstrong always had the radio on in Home Ec. The very same bands were on the radio tonight. In old MTV videos, the musicians' hair-do's were sprayed into crests and waves. Now those styles seemed as ornate and foolish as powdered wigs. Though Silvia had long ago accepted that she would never be as tall or thin as the women in those videos, somewhere deep inside, that hard, sexy aesthetic lingered as ideal.

Now that the pattern was cut out, she had to pin it onto the fabric. She pulled pins out of her pincushion and began sticking them through the pattern and into the black linen. She used the chalk to outline the pattern, then took out the pins. The tissue paper pattern drifted under the table. She cut out the pieces of fabric. There were only three parts, a front, a back, and a long rectangle that with some pressing and pinning and turning right-side-in would become a belt. If Annie was a different woman, Silvia could ask Annie to take charge of the belt, but Annie was not that woman. Right now Annie was smoking a cigarette while doing Pilates on the kitchen floor.

Silvia wanted another glass of wine, but it was getting late, and her hands were feeling more like pieces of sculpture than functioning tools. She held the two big pieces of fabric together and pushed pins down the side where the seam would be. The dress looked more and more like a giant triangle. While Annie crunched herself into a V on the floor, Silvia wondered about the wisdom of wearing a triangle to her tenth anniversary dinner. She wanted to look as good or better than she did on her wedding day, which was impossible, but did she have to try and make herself look terrible? She knew John wasn't even thinking about the dinner, and wouldn't until tomorrow night, when he would pull out his one good pair of pants, a decent shirt, and a sports coat ten minutes before the babysitter arrived.

Silvia poured herself another glass of wine. She bummed one of Annie's cigarettes. "In high school I had a Home Ec teacher named Ms. Armstrong. I don't know if I can sew without her."

Annie stopped exercising to listen. This was the wonderful thing about Annie: she immediately looked so happy to hear a story, sitting cross legged on the kitchen floor with her bottle of lemonade in one hand and her cigarette in the other. "Remind me. When did you graduate?"

"1986. Ms. Armstrong was there to advise, take measurements, do the tricky pleats and tucks, or reconfigure and re-conceive when the zipper wouldn't lie flat."

"Is she still alive?"

"She wasn't old, Annie. She must have only been in her thirties twenty years ago." For a moment Silvia wondered if she could Google Ms. Armstrong and email her for help. "I heard she retired, though, and moved to Florida with Brady."

"Who's Brady?"

"Her common-law husband. He was a Vietnam Vet." In high school Silvia had been impressed by these facts about Brady, though back then she didn't know much about Vietnam and didn't know exactly what "common law" meant. "I thought Ms. Armstrong was so beautiful and independent. She wore stuff like white pumps and drop-waist mini-skirts and taffeta shirts with metallic thread."

"It sounds terrible!"

"I know! But back then it looked great. One day after school, I saw a man picking her up in an old truck."

"Brady?"

"Yeah. He had long brown hair and a scraggly beard. His truck was splattered with dirt."

"Was she wearing the pumps?"

"Yes, and a crazy geometric dress with shoulder pads. She clambered into the truck, and Brady drove off without even kissing her hello. It seemed so pathetic."

"How fascinating," said Annie, blowing a tiny smoke ring that drifted toward the sink. "How come?"

"I think I thought her glamour protected her."

"Ah," said Annie knowingly as she reached up to the counter to retrieve the ashtray.

"The next day I went late to Home Ec. Ms. Armstrong was working with a group of girls I knew needed the credit to graduate, but at that point I had too many credits. I just had this incredible vision of myself, totally confident, wearing a black dress and walking down the street. I was making all these Vogue dresses. I was going to college. The other girls had taken the sewing class three or four times. They were making baby blankets and pillows! They all had serious boyfriends. No boys were even looking at me then."

"You were jealous?"

"I never felt jealous of them. Their boyfriends took auto shop and spent all their money decking out their cars. I thought of them as 'GED material,' even though all of them actually graduated with regular high school diplomas!"

Annie laughed and took a sip of lemonade.

"What a total snob I was back then," said Silvia, stubbing out the cigarette. It had made her dizzy. "I thought I was so different. I thought I was so much better than those girls in my class who were already planning their weddings and deciding how many kids they wanted."

"How many kids did you want?"

"Kids belonged to a distant future I couldn't even imagine." Silvia stood and flicked the iron on to steam.

Annie was kneeling now. She lit another cigarette. "How could you know?"

"How could I know what?" Silvia sat at the sewing machine, lowered the needle into the fabric, and gave the foot pedal a small amount of pressure. At last, she was sewing. The machine whirred, joining the two pieces of fabric together. When the iron was hot, she would press open the seam.

"Do you think this was inevitable?" Annie said, waving her cigarette around the kitchen.

Silvia pushed the fabric under the needle. "I don't know."

"I've been thinking about doing it again." Annie's voice was sad.

"Doing what?" Silvia asked, trying to keep the fabric straight. If it slipped off center, the seam wouldn't lie flat.

"Killing myself."

"Oh, no," Silvia said. She took her foot off the pedal and looked at Annie. "I thought you were better."

Still on her knees, Annie smiled wryly. Behind her appeared Emily, the oldest of the triplets by fifteen minutes.

"I was better," Annie said. "And now I'm not."

Emily was wearing only her underwear. She walked past Annie into the kitchen. "Why was Annie better and now she's not? Why is Annie here?"

"Hey, Emily!" Annie sounded genuinely happy to see Emily, and Silvia understood. Emily awake in the kitchen felt exciting, as if her arrival could give them something they needed.

"What are you doing up?" Silvia asked. Until this moment, she hadn't noticed that the room was filled with smoke.

Emily shrugged. Her underwear was printed with small yellow flowers, and aside from her long brown hair, it was the only obviously feminine thing about her. The rest of her body was as flat and straight as a boy's. Her pajamas were clenched in her fist. She lifted them over her head and began swirling them around in the air like a whip.

"Be careful!" Silvia said. She watched Annie's face flip to another channel. Annie's face was suddenly shining with excitement. What a dangerous room they were in. The iron was hot. Lodged in a wooden block on the countertop, eight steak knives gleamed. The razor blade Silvia used to remove the gummy residue of scotch tape sat on the windowsill.

"Where are the scissors?" Emily asked. "My feet are sweating."

"Why do you need the scissors?" Silvia asked, realizing too late that she was handing them over.

Jane and Charlotte stumbled into the kitchen, blinking in the light. "What are we doing?" Jane asked. Charlotte looked like she was still sleeping.

Emily was kneeling on the floor, spreading out her pajamas. She looked over her shoulder at her sisters. "We're cutting off our feet."

Charlotte looked miserable to hear the news, but Jane unzipped her pajamas and stepped out of them immediately. "Good idea," she said. "Why is Annie smoking when it's bad for you?"

"Think of it as a dream," Annie said. "This isn't really happening."

Jane raised her eyebrows.

Charlotte, apparently resigned to the plan, tugged at the zipper on her pajamas. It was stuck. She moved in front of Annie and pushed out her belly. Annie clenched the cigarette in her teeth and pulled the fleece free. "Thanks," said Charlotte, and finished unzipping. Now that she was more awake, she looked cheery. She shrugged her pajamas to the floor and laughed. "Oops. I forgot my underwear."

Jane stood behind Emily, who was still bent over the floor, cutting. Jane's underwear was printed across the front with the sparkly word *Sunday* even though it was Friday. Naked, Charlotte stood in line behind Jane.

"Need help?" Annie asked, blowing a big smoke ring.

Charlotte and Jane watched it float above the refrigerator. They looked at each other and grinned. "Cool!" they said in unison.

*Quit it*, mouthed Silvia.

*Relax*, mouthed Annie.

"No," Emily muttered. "I don't need any help." She stood up, handed the scissors to Jane, and stepped back into her pajamas, ankle bones delicate beneath the ragged fleece. There were no calluses or plantar warts or varicose veins on her feet. Her heels were so close to her toes. "May I please have some milk?" she asked. Her voice was so grave that Silvia had to laugh.

"Very polite," Annie murmured.

"Aren't they beautiful?" Silvia couldn't help asking.

"Almost too beautiful to believe," Annie said. "Like a dream."

All three girls looked at Annie and scowled.

"C-ut! C-ut!" Charlotte began to chant impatiently, giving the word two syllables. Jane finished her pajamas and handed the scissors over her shoulder to Charlotte, who knelt gently on the floor, her naked body thicker than her sisters' and as simple as a shell.

Silvia got the milk from the refrigerator. The cool air felt good on her face. Maybe she should drink some milk. No. She got out three glasses and filled each half-way.

"More," Emily said. "We're really thirsty."

"Yes," Jane said, nodding.

"Please," Charlotte remembered to add as she happily stepped back into her now-footless pajamas and zipped herself up.

Silvia watched Annie watch the girls drink their milk. Their six pink feet crowded the linoleum next to the refrigerator like a small flock of creatures who might transform at any moment into something entirely new.

When they finished their milk, they began exploring.

"What are you doing?" Jane asked, running her hand

along the top of the sewing machine. Charlotte was feeling the fabric between her fingers. Emily was pulling pins from the tomato.

"Making a dress. It's time to get back to bed," Silvia said. She wanted them out of the kitchen before they really woke up and started asking to use the sewing machine, please, just this once, just for a little while....

"Why are you making a dress?" Charlotte asked.

"I don't know, exactly," Silvia answered. She couldn't say to her daughters, I love you all, I wanted you all, but I didn't think I'd have to go through it, I thought I could elude, I thought I could rise above, circumvent, not get snagged, not get lumpy, not get bumpy. I thought if I was smart enough, skinny enough, fast enough—

"You know," Annie said, her voice wise and warm, "she's just making it for fun."

"Yeah," Jane said.

"Tuck us in, please," Emily commanded over her shoulder as she led the other girls out of the kitchen.

"I'll be there in a minute," Silvia said. "Go on up." She wanted to thank Annie. She wanted to try and explain.

"I'm tired, too," Annie yawned, and put out her hand.

Silvia pulled her off the kitchen floor, led her into the living room, and handed her a pillow from the rocking chair. "Lie down on the couch and take a nap."

Annie stretched out. "Thank you for letting me come over. I know you have sewing to do."

"Shut up," said Silvia. "I'll bring you a blanket from the girls' room." She was worried about leaving Annie alone, but it would just take a minute.

The stairs creaked as Silvia ascended. It was too quiet upstairs. The girls were probably hiding, she thought, and she would have to find them, and then chase them, and then yell at them to get back into bed. But no: in their room, the girls were all, astonishingly, asleep. Charlotte and Jane were huddled under the covers in Charlotte's bed. Emily was in her own bed, mouth open, eyes fluttering. Silvia resisted the urge to touch Emily's bare feet. She pulled a blanket up to Emily's chin, grabbed the comforter off Jane's empty bed, and walked back downstairs to the living room.

Annie was sitting on the couch, hugging the pillow. Her face was wistful in the light spilling out of the kitchen.

"I thought you were tired," Silvia said.

"I thought I was, too."

"You want more salami? Another lemonade?"

Annie shook her head, stood, and followed Silvia back into the kitchen.

"Remember what the shaman said?"

"What?" Silvia was trying not to worry about the dress. There it was, still in pieces.

"We already have everything we need."

Silvia rolled her eyes. "It's just that I had this idea of

a dress," she said, sitting back down at the sewing machine. The thread had come free from the needle and the fabric was hanging off the side of the table.

"An ideal, right?" Annie lowered herself back to the floor. She pulled her knees up to her chest and stuck her arms out straight along the sides of her body. "I'm going to do another boat pose. Work on my abs."

Silvia rethreaded the needle and re-centered the fabric. "Maybe it's hopeless."

"Look," Annie said. "All these little feet." She gathered a few fleece footies from the triplets' pajamas in each hand. It looked like the muscles in Annie's stomach were beginning to quiver, but still she kept the V of her boat pose. She shook the footies vigorously. "I'm your cheerleader, okay? Go, Silvia! Sew that dress!"

"Okay, okay," Silvia said. There were still hours until morning. She rethreaded the needle, repositioned the fabric, and finished sewing the seam. Now to iron it flat.

When she looked up, Annie was curled on her side on the kitchen floor, sleeping, wearing the footies on her hands like mittens.

# FOUR

JELLY SMEARS across your cheek. The couch is a good place to wipe your nose. You won't wear anything but sweatpants. You're a big boy. Everyone says this about you every day, every time they see you, even if it's more than twice. He's so big! They whisper it to your mom so you can hear it. He's a beautiful boy, says your mom. Very smart and a joker too. Calls himself Storm.

YOUR BROTHER hits you. You notice he does not like you. It seems to you he likes you less now than he used to when you were little. You tell your mom. Your mom says it isn't true. She said it's always been hard for your brother to have a brother and that it's actually better now that you are big. You say you aren't big. She asks if you're still little and you say medium. You hit your brother when you can. After breakfast you hit him on the head with your fist until your mom sees and says stop you're hurting him and puts you and your brother in separate rooms. Your brother always hits you first. Your mom says there's no hitting in your family.

YOU GET THE TV room for time out. You howl for awhile until you see your Transformer magazine. You bring it to your mom. Your mom is cleaning out the bird cage. Yuck, she says. They poop a lot. The two parent birds laid eggs. The eggs hatched. Now the babies are trying to fly. They get stuck behind the water dish and look like they only have one leg. You got to name the first two babies: Spike and Hiss. You hold up your magazine and say I want you to read me this. Your mom says no, you are in time out. Go back until you hear the timer.

(THE TIMER is on the microwave and one time when your mom took a rest in your bottom bunk for a few minutes before it was time to pick up your brother from school she really fell asleep. You went into the kitchen, pulled a chair over to the microwave and hit the timer button. You turned it off. When your mom woke up she said I think I fell asleep. You giggled. She went into the kitchen to check the timer and yelled Oh shit! You were late. You had to drive and you were happy because your mom had to put your shoes and socks on and you got to take the car instead of walk. Also your brother was crying when you picked him up because he thought you weren't coming.)

You NEED to poop. Your mom makes you wipe now, all by yourself. No help. She says it's enough already. Now you have to wash your hands. Sometimes it's hard to reach the toilet paper. It rolls away. Or you use too much. Your mom has to use a plunger or pull toilet paper out with her hand and she gets mad. Flush a few times, she says. Poop butt stinky fart is your favorite song. It's only for home, not for preschool. Your mom says it isn't funny. You say you and your brother think it's funny. Your friends think it's funny, too. Sometimes your mom laughs and sometimes she says enough and sometimes she yells quit it! Your mom has a special word called LIMIT and that means really stop.

SNEAKERS AND SOCKS are a big problem. Your sneakers do not light up. There are no Transformers on your sneakers. The socks hurt. They hurt. They don't go on right. Your mom won't help you anymore. You lie on the floor and howl about the socks. You throw them all, find a car to push, and stop howling. Your mom puts on lipstick in the bathroom. It takes a long time. You don't like your mom in the bathroom with the door shut. You say it's too scary. You yell for your mom but she doesn't answer and you don't bang on the door anymore because that is how your big brother got his fingers caught and your mom kicked the wall and made a hole and cried. When your mom comes out of the bathroom she says she doesn't want to help you with your socks and shoes but now it's late, so she helps you with your socks and makes you do the rest.

You drop your big brother at his school first and then your mom leaves you at preschool. She plays a game and then she says goodbye. You cry. Your mom hugs you. You tell your mom you don't want her to leave. Your mom says look, your friends are here. Cole is playing blocks. He's not my friend, you say. You say you don't like school. You used to like it, says your mom. You say you never did. Your mom hugs you one more time and says see you right after lunch, remember you have a Gogurt for lunch? Oh yeah you say and stop crying for a minute. Your mom leaves.

After preschool you go to a new store with your mom. A woman helps you, but your mom does not. You get new sneakers and socks. You get to pick them out but not totally. The sneakers light up but there are no Transformers. Your mom said no Transformers because those weren't good for your feet and no Bionicles because they were too much money. The woman shows you a mirror so you can see the light-ups. You wear them home. You race up and down the block with your mom and you always win.

WHEN IT'S TIME to pick up your brother from first grade the new sneakers hurt. The new socks hurt too. You throw your sneakers across the living room. One of them hits your mom. Your mom says she really feels like spanking you! You start crying. You say that really hurts your feelings. You put on sandals even though it's cold out.

YOU PLAY on the playground. Your big brother plays with his friends. Today they let you play and you only get pushed over two times and it doesn't even hurt. Your mother sits in a sunny spot and hands out pretzels to kids that say please. Some days she talks to other parents. Today she sits against a wall all by herself and watches you play.

IN THE DARK TV room (your mom puts the light on but your brother always turns it off when she closes the door) you fall asleep during "ZOOM." To wake you up your mom gives you a lollypop. She says if you sleep now forget tonight. The lollypop is gone. You must have eaten it but you don't remember. You are cold. Your mom gets you another shirt. Your dad is at a meeting. That means he's not eating dinner with you. At the table you get mashed sweet potatoes. You yell you hate sweet potatoes. You want mashed white! Yum yum, says your brother. He licks his lips. Thanks mom, these are very good! You push the bowl of mashed sweet potatoes almost off the table. You are still chilly and your mom gets you your bathrobe and puts it on too tight. Too tight! Your mom says take a deep breath. Is she talking to you? You cry and yell until the ravioli is ready and then you eat the ravioli. It's good. You like ravioli.

As SOON AS your father gets home your mother says she's going for a walk to get some milk. You want to know why your mother is crying. Why would she cry about milk?

# SPECIAL ABILITY

FRANCES THOUGHT motherhood must be a gradual transition, though getting pregnant happened quickly and Louis dwindled from husband to ex in minutes. She asked her therapy group how long it took to turn a woman into a mom. Individual answers varied. Physically on average, nine months. But psychically? Some women said it was immediate, automatic. Others said major alterations never stuck: they popped the kid out and resumed their former identities. One mother declared permanent transformation and lifted her shirt to display the evidence: folds of belly skin, deflated, post-nursing breasts. The therapy group came to a consensus: get to know a real kid. The local elementary school needed reading buddies. Frances knew nothing about buddies, but she knew about books. She managed the children's section of a bookstore. Children's books didn't muddy good and evil or go on and on about nothing. Magic occurred easily and villains got what they deserved.

MJ, THE MOM KNEELING next to Frances in the elementary school storage closet, looked born to the role of mother. Her hair bounced from her head in get-the-job-done curls.

"I'm pregnant." Frances offered this statement of fact.

"Congratulations! I have three." MJ's face, arms, and legs were thin, but her belly looked preg-nant. Since she didn't mention a fourth kid on the way, neither did Frances. Either MJ could not get enough of the mom metamorphosis, or her abdominal muscles were shot.

In Frances' experience, mothers were not only flabby, they were incredibly self-involved. It was at the packed shelf of parenting books (located conveniently next to the children's books section) that Frances arrived at this conclusion. When pregnant women walked into the door of the bookstore, they gravitated toward the parenting shelf like chubby magnets. It didn't appear to change after they had their babies, either. Mothers pushing strollers became even more self-obsessed. Month after month they purchased material about mothering. Of course this happened: historians reading history, doctors reading medical reports; but since when was mothering a profession? But perhaps working in a bookstore wasn't a profession either.

Even before she got pregnant, Frances noticed fliers on billboards all over town: mommy playgroups, mommy book clubs, mommy knitting circles, mommy yoga. There were even biker-mom-joy-rides while the kids were at school. Frances had a word for this phenomenon, for these mom-crazy women: momaholics. There was never any evidence of dadaholism in the fathers Frances observed. Dads appeared to wing it. Becoming a mom seemed joining a club and Frances wasn't sure a) whether she wanted a membership and b) whether one would be granted.

"Let's train you," said MJ. She plucked a skinny book from a plastic tub full of books and Frances wondered why she even listened to her therapy group.

THE THERAPY GROUP contained an odd collection of women, aged thirty to fifty, whose pieces weren't quite fitting. They sat in a circle on the carpeted floor of the therapist's office, which was located at the edge of a strip mall. Some women sat cross-legged. Others stretched their legs out long into the center of the circle. Rain often rolled down the big plate glass windows that looked out onto a small patch of woods. It was a surprisingly beautiful, green, and tangled view.

IN THE STORAGE CLOSET, MJ held up a book. A cartoon dog, leash hanging from its mouth, drooled on the cover.

"Pictures give context clues." She flipped through the book, making sure that Frances saw each illustration. She read the title out loud, pretending to be a kid who stammered: "*The Dog*." Then she stumbled through the whole sentence. "The dog wants to go for a walk." That one sentence comprised the entire book. It was no wonder some kids didn't want to learn how to read.

MJ found a marker in the plastic bin and copied the sentence onto a long strip of paper while Frances tried to pay attention. It didn't matter for tutoring, but she wouldn't be living in the neighborhood much longer. Now that Louis had moved out, Frances would have to sell the house.

MJ snipped the paper strip with the sentence *The dog wants to go for a walk* into individual words using blunt rubber handled scissors. Then she grabbed a blue folder out of the plastic tub and placed it flat on the linoleum.

"Now it's time for the child to put the sentence back together." The cashmere sweater MJ wore made Frances sweat even though she was wearing nothing but jeans and a t-shirt. Surging pregnancy hormones made her feel immersed in a chemical bath.

"These kids need boundaries." MJ picked up *The* and placed it at the edge of the blue folder. "They need a frame." She placed *dog* after *The*. "They're—they need more time." MJ omitted the word slow, but it appeared in Frances' mind, written in her dead grandmother's flowery cursive. Next to *dog*, MJ placed *wants to go for a walk*.

"After they put the sentence back together, have them read it to you, and put the pieces in the envelope. They take the sentence home to practice." MJ waved a small manila envelope in the air.

Frances was changing her mind about tutoring; it was boring and she was hungry. She could be sitting with her feet up in her kitchen right now, eating a buttery English muffin and re-reading *A Series of Unfortunate Events*.

"Frankie's waiting for you in the hallway outside the first grade classroom," said MJ. Lemony Snicket would have to wait. Frances slipped *The Dog* inside the blue folder and went to find Frankie.

SOME OF THE WOMEN in her therapy group hated their jobs, some hated their spouses, some hated their mothers; they all hated something. *Discover what you want*, the therapist intoned. *Discover what you need and make it happen*. Frances knew she wasn't at that level yet. She didn't make things happen. Things happened to her. Her "discoveries" tended to look like this: she was pregnant and Louis was leaving her for another woman.

"Now what?" Frances looked around at the therapy

group, all of whom looked back at her. "Do I want his baby? I want to kill Louis." Many of the women nodded. One way-too-thin woman started to cry. The therapist frowned thoughtfully. Encouraged by their attention, Frances continued her monologue:

"When I confronted Louis about cheating on me, I was chopping green pepper. I love green pepper, but I hate chopping it, hate having to cut around the white part, hate shaking off all the little seeds. When Louis said he was leaving I didn't run at him with the knife. I fantasized about stashing the knife under my pillow so I could slit his throat while he was sleeping. Then I rinsed the knife, cut a red onion and sprinkled salt on the lettuce. I wished for poison dust. I fantasized about Louis writhing to his death after one bite of salad.

Why did I think we were going to eat dinner together? Why did I think he was going to sleep next to me in our bed? Why so many tactical mistakes?" Frances began to hyperventilate and the therapist handed her a paper bag just big enough for a school lunch.

"Well?" As usual, the therapist turned to the group. Frances peeked above the paper sack. The circle of women smiled sadly. Over time each woman's issues had become evident, which was, according to the therapist, *entirely the point of the group*. More than one woman drank when she was depressed. Others ate too much or not at all. A couple of women picked up men in bars or over the internet. Three women were known to berate themselves silently but nonstop, and one beat up her husband. Frances knew that she was the woman who retreated into fantasy when real life became too painful. She read. She read a lot. She didn't mention that it was lucky she didn't have any poison the night Louis left, because if she had, she would have eaten it herself.

FRANKIE WASN'T EXACTLY hiding, but he wasn't eagerly waiting for his tutoring session either. He was crouched down behind a plastic chair pushed next to his student desk, drawing on the chair's stainless steel legs with a pencil. Frances wondered if she should she squat down to his level.

"It won't work," she said, deciding to stand taller than usual. "Pencil won't work on metal."

"Metal is more powerfuller than pencil." Frankie examined the chair leg and smiled up at Frances.

"Guess what," said Frances. "Our names both start with *F*."

"I know the F-word," said Frankie. He slipped into the school desk and began doodling on the wooden desk top with his pencil. "Pencil is more powerfuller than wood," he whispered to himself.

Frances sat down in the plastic chair and slid a blue folder under his pencil.

"Paper is smarter than wood," said Frances. "My name

is Frances, like in *Bread and Jam for Frances*. Remember those books? Frances is that porcupine or hedgehog or something, remember?"

"Sonic is a hedgehog." Frankie looked enormously pleased. When he smiled, Frances saw that his teeth were a variety of shapes and sizes.

"Who's Sonic?"

Frankie didn't answer. Instead he opened the blue folder and pulled out *The Dog*. His facial expression was difficult to decipher. *The Dog* was a cheap little stapled together book.

"Can you read me the title?" Next time she tutored, Frances would definitely smuggle in something good by Shel Silverstein or Roald Dahl.

Frankie was poking his pencil up his nose.

"I work at a bookstore," said Frances. "I can bring you good books."

"We go to libary at school," said Frankie, leaving out the r in library. "They rent you computer games for free."

"Do you like to read?"

"I like *Captain Underpants*." A solid half inch of Frankie's pencil was no longer visible.

"You only get one nose," said Frances. "Don't poke a hole in it."

"Do you like *Captain Underpants*?"

"Not really," said Frances, reluctantly admitting the truth. Weren't children like dogs? Couldn't they smell a lie? *Captain Underpants* was one of the children section's strongest sellers. Written to look as though penned by an ignorant kid, it was full of misspelled words and potty jokes. In the bookstore, moms sighed and moaned, but bought it anyway. Dads actually liked it. On rainy Saturdays, dads came into the bookstore with their kids and read *Captain Underpants* out loud. Then they'd leave, without buying anything. Moms never did that. Moms almost always bought at least one book out of guilt.

"What else do you like?" asked Frances.

"*Yu-Gi-Oh*! I have the most powerfullest attack and defense." Frankie leaned forward and pulled out what looked like a baseball card from the back pocket of his jeans. The card lay flat in his palm. He shifted his hand from side to side and the metallic figure—a dragon? A devil holding a sword?—glinted in the fluorescent hallway light. "Special ability." Frankie's voice was barely a whisper.

"It's some kind of card game?" Frances looked at her watch. Ten of their thirty tutoring minutes were already gone.

"On FOX," said Frankie, still whispering, as though television stations were another major secret.

On the wall above their heads, a shrill bell rang.

"Fire!" Frankie yelled. He leapt up from his desk. The first grade door swung open and the teacher strode out in a fuzzy red dress and high heeled boots.

"Fire drill," the teacher corrected. She looked twenty-three. A giant claw gripped her twisted hair. Frankie pushed for a spot in line as kids surged into the hallway.

"Bye," said Frances, but Frankie had already disappeared into the mob. She picked up his blue folder. Beneath it was his card. In his rush, he'd forgotten it.

Frances slid the card into the back pocket of her jeans so she could return it to him during their next session. She felt light-headed, tingly. She better not be coming down with the flu. The Sci Fi manager at the bookstore had warned her about *vile kid germs*.

Frances made her way through the crowded hallways and exited the school, then ran across the street through the rain, splashing on purpose through several deep puddles.


INSIDE, HER SOON-TO-BE-SOLD house was darker than outside, because recently she'd stopped turning on the lights. To save money, she explained, though her therapy group suggested she didn't want to see the house she shared with Louis become empty. Louis had taken all his stuff except for a few boxes he said he'd pick up sometime when he was in the neighborhood. He even took the puppy that had failed to pull them back together.

In the living room, Frances yanked off her boots and wet socks. She pulled Frankie's card out of her pocket to make sure it hadn't gotten wet. When she looked at it, she felt dizzy. She couldn't see the words on it very well; the writing was in tiny print. The strange devil-dragon's eyes looked directly into hers. *Darkness is stronger than light*, thought Frances. She took a deep breath to clear her head and returned the card to her back pocket.

In the kitchen she sliced an English muffin with a knife. *Metal is stronger than bread.* When she put the English muffin in the toaster, she wondered how hot the toaster would have to get before it melted. She imagined hot lava dripping slowly down the cabinets. The English muffin popped up. She buttered it. *Heat is more powerful than butter.* She took a bite. *Teeth are more powerful than bread.*

Frances got the sugar bowl off the kitchen table and dumped a mountain onto her English muffin. The sugar felt gritty in her mouth. Some of her teeth felt as small and smooth as mini M&Ms, others were giant and ridged like potato chips. Two teeth were loose, several were missing. Frances pushed the wobbly ones around with her finger until she tasted blood. She picked a hard booger out of her nose and flicked it, then picked up the plastic bag of English muffins from the counter and started swinging. The muffins smashed against the cabinets. The bag broke. Pieces of muffin flew all over the kitchen. *Cabinets are more powerful than plastic. Cabinets are more powerful than bread. Everything is more powerful than bread!*

Frances had to pee really badly; she was going to

have an accident. Tears trickled into her mouth. She ran down the hallway to the bathroom. She flipped the toilet seat up with a bang and pointed her rubbery little penis at the toilet. Most of the pee hit the floor. Weak gray light came through the bathroom window; Frances watched the last drops of pee make rings of water in the toilet. Then she shook her penis until nothing more came out. *Pee is smellier than water*. She couldn't say her l right. She didn't flush.

Outside, rain was still falling. The sky grew darker. A flash of lightning lit the living room. Frances saw the empty doggy bed pushed behind the couch. In his haste to abandon her, Louis had forgotten it. Thunder rumbled. Frances jumped into the bed, turning round in circles repeatedly. The flannel smelled good. Every time it thundered, she panted, whined, and shook.

A knock at the front door. A key turning the lock. Frances got up on all fours. Her ears quivered, her nails scratched the wood floor. The front door opened. She knew what she wanted. Louis! She smelled Louis.

"Louis! Louis!" she barked. She ran to him and jumped up, hoping he would rub her ears.

"Quit it," said Louis, brushing past her. "Don't beg; I'm never coming back." Frances whimpered and returned to the doggy bed. Louis went in and out through the front door several times, carrying boxes, dripping water. "This is my last box." The door slammed. His car started. It peeled out, screeching.

Frances howled until her throat hurt. She licked water off the floor. It didn't taste like Louis. She stretched up and balanced her front paws against the couch where the Sunday comics were spread across the cushions. She knew Charlie Brown, Luanne, Hagar, Dilbert; they all talked into bubbles. But what were they saying? She could pick out letters one at a time, but she couldn't put them together. There was an *F. F* for Frances. *F* for Frankie. *F* for the F-word. Frances didn't know what the F-word was, but she knew it was important. She would go back to school and find Frankie. He would know.

She pulled her rubber boots back on without socks and ran across the street, sloshing through the irresistible puddles. Yellow light glowed through the glass in the school's front doors. The brass handles were heavy and cold. Frances pulled as hard as she could. The warm dry air inside the school sucked her toward the storage closet. She found the blue folder on the shelf where she had left it. The deserted hallways were filled with chanted multiplication tables, alphabets in Spanish, coughs, and claps.

The first grade door was open. Frances stood in the doorway, holding the blue folder against her chest. The teacher was writing a secret code on the board: *2 2 2 4 2 2 2 4 2 2 __ 4*

"We're learning about patterns," she said when she saw Frances. "You know, fill in the blank?"

Frankie grabbed his pencil. As he walked by his teacher, he reached out and brushed his hand against her wooly dress.

"No touching other people's bodies," his teacher said sternly.

Frankie blushed and tucked his hand behind his back. In the hallway he slid into his small desk. Frances sat down next to him in the plastic chair. Frankie stopped his finger before it began burrowing up his nose.

"Where is it?" he demanded. "I want my card back."

Frances slid the card out of her pocket and held it in her palm. It was just a card: thick flat paper, a rectangle with rounded edges. She didn't want to return the card to Frankie, but he plucked it from her hand. She didn't want to slide the *s* back next to the *he*. She wasn't dizzy anymore; she didn't have a penis. The deep need to break everything was gone.

Frankie kissed the card before pushing it directly into his back pocket. "Don't be sad," he said. "You can buy these at the supermarket." He opened his reading folder, pulled out the chintzy little book, *The Dog*, and began sounding out the words.

"Look at the pictures," Frances reminded him. "Don't forget about context clues." Her breasts felt heavy again, like sadness she couldn't shake. She remembered the F-word now. It had to do with being touched. Her secret code was mysterious and hidden, like the baby growing in her belly. She would teach Frankie to read, but it would take years and years for her to figure out one simple sentence. *What I need is* _____.

# TEETH

By the time the dentist arrived in the cubicle, Darla's back hurt from sitting in the chair. The hygienist had already suggested whitening, straightening, and a night guard. Apparently, Darla was grinding in her sleep. In just ten minutes and one personal interaction, she had gone from feeling reasonably well-kempt to feeling like Yuk Mouth from that old cartoon, or Frankenstein, or a hillbilly woman. And she was paying a babysitter for this.

True, she did not have dental insurance and tried to get by on one cleaning a year, but she fully embraced her greater personal responsibility by brushing at least three times a day with baking soda/fluoride toothpaste, in addition to vigorous nightly flossing. Sometimes her husband fell asleep before she even made it into the bedroom. Sometimes she wanted him to—she wasn't in the mood to even talk. Other times she hustled the flossing, or (in truth) skipped it, dug up some lingerie and had sex like a maniac with her husband, like the two people they used to be before the boys came and everything got very busy and very serious or very busy and very silly. It didn't happen all at once. And it wasn't always easy to tell what was serious and what was silly. A screaming child (or parent) could start out serious and then get silly. With the bank book, it happened the other way around: first silly and then so serious they were afraid to even open it.

One boy had not been so drastic. She had worked part-time for money and painted during the hours when he napped, brought him to cafés and shared potato soup from her spoon, and tooled around town with him in a plastic seat on the back of her bicycle. It was true that when she was with her son, men no longer hit on her (she noticed this when, by chance alone, men did hit on her—though on those occasions she felt sure there was baby puke on her coat, or that maybe the men did, in fact, need to know the time) but she didn't miss the Male Gaze that much. Men weren't even that interesting, usually, unless they were very interesting, and that felt dangerous. She avoided those particular men when infrequently she met one.

Down at the end of the dentist chair, her feet rested on the thick plastic mat. She wore the pink-and-white-striped suede sneakers she bought six months ago, days after her thirty-fifth birthday, in a vague effort to both console herself and retain some aura of hipness. The birthday itself had been disappointing—too much like any other rainy autumn Portland day, except for a few phone calls she missed while making runs to school and the store. The evening started off okay, with take-out Thai food and a store-bought cake Tom brought home. After they sang, she opened her presents: Tom gave her a subscription to *Art News* and tickets to an existential play; the boys, body lotion and shampoo; and her parents sent a glittery pink card with a check for fifty dollars. *Happy Birthday!* the card insisted, *This is just for you! We know how hard it is.* Thirty minutes after the presents were opened, Tom said he wasn't feeling well and went to lie down, while the boys started acting nuts from the sugar in the cake. Darla did her best to keep her sense of humor intact while the boys did their usual pee, brush teeth, and wash hands and face routine. She read them books they chose without paying attention to the words. Instead, she was giving herself a little pep talk, reminding herself to be thankful that the boys were happy and healthy, that she and Tom were healthy (relatively), that they had food on the table and a roof over their heads. She forced herself to think of the real troubles of people in Iraq and Liberia and Nigeria, and also Israel and Palestine.

Tom's flu lasted forty-eight hours. It wasn't horrible

and messy—he just stayed in bed. The hour he was feeling better, Darla drove straight to the mall. There was no way she would get to the little shoe boutiques she used to frequent way back when. (They were only open during the day and she had the CHILDREN and they DIDN'T LIKE TO SHOP and she couldn't AFFORD those shoes anymore, anyway.) Darla parked next to Sears and walked through quickly; she would not sink so low as to buy sneakers from Sears. Part of her wanted to see someone she knew and could talk to, and part of her didn't—she knew she would come across as strange and desperate. At least that's how she felt. It occurred to her that she could get a job at the mall in the evenings to make a little extra money, but it would be very little, and when would she have any time with Tom? But maybe that would be good.

Darla bought the suede sneakers on sale from a man in a referee uniform. "I'm going to wear them home," she said, and the referee shrugged—it wasn't his call. On the drive home she kept the shoe box containing her old sneakers next to her on the passenger seat. These new sneakers spoke to her heart, a classic style redone in pink suede, as fresh and as witty as she would like herself to be.

In the fluorescent light of the dentist's office, the sneakers now appeared grayish instead of pink, mottled from dirt and rain. A dark smudge on the thigh of Darla's jeans made her want to lean over and sniff, but the dentist entered the room. She just had to hope it wasn't poop. For the past week her little boy had been potty training ambivalently. He didn't mind peeing in the potty, but unless she watched him constantly, he pooped in his underwear (printed with dinosaurs) and yelled, *Mom! I pooped!* Then she swooped down on him and rushed him into the bathroom.

"It's hard to walk," he said crossly.

"That's why we poop in the potty."

They scowled at each other and then she got to work getting the poop off his body while he complained. "Ow! You're hurting me!" His voice was full of indignation.

In the hallway outside the bathroom, his six-year-old brother kept up a running commentary on the entire process. "P.U.! It stinks in there. Yup, that's how she does it when she cleans you off. It always hurts."

This was a moment when having two children felt like a bad idea. Whenever she felt stressed and double-teamed, however, she reminded herself of women who had three kids, or four—or of her own mother who had had seven, and her grandmother who had had twelve—and tried to stop her sniveling about two measly kids, and to keep her sense of humor. Potty training was absurd. She should forget about painting (it was so tempting to stop being an artist, to stop trying to be an artist) and do a children's book about poop. No one seemed to understand or want her paintings anyway. People love children's books and they love poop. (Her older brother worked at a museum of contemporary art in New York City, and for a while the museum exhibited what was essentially a poop machine made by a Japanese artist. Her brother said it was really popular; in Japan, it had apparently been the most well-attended art exhibit ever. People could feed the machine bananas and beans and then watch the poop come out. Her brother said it smelled just like real poop, too.)

The air in the bathroom was close and smelly. Darla wanted to open the window, but didn't dare let go of her three-year-old. She wasn't trying to be rough, but he was trying to squirm away and the poop was sticky. He was looking at her with hate on his beautiful smooth face and she wished she was at a time and place in her life where she didn't interact so much with poop.

"At least she wipes you," his older brother was saying outside the door. "She makes me do it myself."

"You're six!" Darla yelled. There was poop everywhere: bum, legs, underwear, pants, shirt, the outside of the potty, the floor. Hours later, after scouring her little boy, the bathroom and herself, she had noticed a tiny bit of poop way up on the inside of her arm and felt more discouraged by it than disgusted.

That night, her recurring dream had cropped up once again. A giant boy sat on a huge wooden potty/platform yelling, "Wipe me! Wipe me!" and waving an immense wooden spoon (or something) in the air. She was in the dream too, normal sized, or maybe shrunk, climbing up a rickety ladder to the wooden platform covered in dried bird shit.

Waking life was less dramatic but more grinding. She used to wake up early to paint, but because the boys seemed to be telepathically linked to her, they began waking up earlier and earlier too. Her husband did not follow suit. Some mornings she counted the hours until bedtime. Those mornings started at 5:30 a.m. and by 9 a.m. she was thinking about cold brown bottles of beer. Darla lived in fear of the word hobbyist. Painting at night after the children were asleep seemed like a good idea, but proved impossible for her tired and rapidly aging body.

"Hi Darla," said the dentist as she appeared around the bend of cubicle. "Remember me, Dr. Pot? We haven't seen you for a full year." Dr. Pot had a sing song voice that implied Darla wasn't flossing regularly. From previous appointments, Darla knew the dentist's name and had warned herself sternly not to laugh. This was difficult, because she always felt slightly hysterical at the dentist's office. It didn't matter what kind of dentist she went to: new age and no pain, or old school and sadistic. To not laugh, she looked at her ratty sneakers. Dr. Pot wore rimless, slightly tinted safety glasses reminiscent of Jennifer Lopez. Darla couldn't tell Dr. Pot's age, but she seemed young. In theory and practice, Darla supported young medical professionals, though in her heart she would have found an old dentist more reassuring.

She noticed a scab on her right anklebone. Part of being hip had something to do with not wearing socks, or at least it used to—she wasn't really sure about that anymore. Compared to her pre-kids life, she spent almost no time getting dressed or going shopping, yet still felt guilty about her suede sneakers. That's where she was at: guilty for buying sneakers she wore everyday for six months and still thought of as new.

"Let's get started," said Dr. Pot. "Open." Darla complied. "Your teeth start to even out," said Dr. Pot. Cambodian was her first language, and because of this, she had an odd way with English, like she was talking to Darla and at the same time addressing a larger audience. Not that there was anyone else to talk to. The male hygienist Darla liked was either standing behind the dentist where he couldn't be seen, or he had gotten out of the cubicle altogether. Maybe he didn't like Dr. Pot, either. "It happens when you get old," said Dr. Pot. "You grind at night." She smiled and shrugged. Darla wondered if she had meant to say older instead of old, and also wondered if Tom had ever heard her grinding. He never mentioned it. Did Dr. Pot find her sneakers ridiculous? Now she was looking at the x-rays that the hygienist had recommended and then taken when Darla reluctantly assented to them. She always hoped to avoid the x-rays, because they cost eighty-five dollars, and she didn't want the bad news x-rays almost always brought. She was pretty sure she had a cavity: a tooth on the upper left side of her mouth hurt when she bit into anything sweet or cold.

While Dr. Pot looked at the x-rays, Darla wondered if the male hygienist, Matt, remembered her from visit to visit the way she remembered him. Probably not. Still, he seemed to have a good time with her; she was always so nervous at her appointment and laughed so easily at his small jokes that it egged him on to be funnier and funnier, until they both had to take a break so she could stop laughing and he could clean her teeth. He was cute, young, smooth-skinned, and scrubbed clean in a clearly non-hetero way. Together they enjoyed complaining about Portland's rainy season and extolling the big city virtues of New York and Los Angeles. She wondered who Matt hung out with on the weekends, and felt bad about the plaque that built up behind her bottom two front teeth.

"Sorry," she had said after he had hacked away at the spot for several minutes.

"It's a hard spot to floss," he'd reassured her.

"I do try," she wanted to say, but didn't, because she thought she might cry. Plus his hands and scraper were in her mouth. In addition to hysteria, going to the dentist always made her overly emotional.

Dr. Pot was gesturing toward the x-rays up on the light board. Darla had to turn her body around to see them, which strained her lower back. "A kid draws a picture, the teeth are even, but that's not true. The incisors are supposed to be longer than the others." Dr. Pot pointed a metal tool at Darla's x-ray and sighed. "Since you're grinding, you need a night guard. Open." Dr. Pot held glinting instruments over Darla's open mouth and then relaxed her hands back down to her sides. It was odd that Tom never heard her grinding her teeth. She woke up when he snored loudly or when he yelled out during a nightmare. He never woke up during her nightmares—she'd just push close to him and wrap her arms around his body. Darla didn't want a night guard because a) she couldn't afford one and b) she didn't want to jam something into her mouth while she was trying to sleep. People were getting way too crazy about teeth. At her son's school there were two girls with giant metal contraptions on the outside of their mouths. Darla looked around the playground for the parents of these girls but never saw them. Who would do such a thing to their child?

Darla would not consent to be assaulted or manipulated while she slept. She didn't even let the boys climb into her bed anymore in the middle of the night. They were big boys and both night punchers. She and Tom kept sleeping bags and pillows on the floor next to their bed, and called the area "Camp Muddy Waters."

Dr. Pot was not finished with her recommendations. "New whiteners. Great treatments. Many options, really. Brushing not enough. Coffee, chocolate, tea. Yellow teeth make you look old." She let the instruments she was holding in both hands clatter back onto the metal tray. From her pocket she pulled out a little deck of cards that looked like sample squares of linoleum strung together on a keychain. If Darla worked with found objects she might find a use for the squares, but she didn't do that kind of work. She painted.

"Teeth together," said Dr. Pot. She brought the samples up to Darla's mouth. Dr. Pot demonstrated the desired grin. Darla mimicked it, glad not to be instructed to bite down on the linoleum. "We think teeth are white," said Dr. Pot, as she held out a sample card the color of old ivory and then brought it close to Darla's eyes. "This is your color."

The card was too close for Darla's eyes to focus properly, but she knew it was more yellow than was acceptable, though she wondered if Dr. Pot's tinted glasses were making things appear worse than they really were. Every time she went to the dentist it felt like she was getting a bad report card, a fate she never had to suffer as a kid. She shrugged the way she imagined a kid who always got a D in Math might.

"You had your wisdom teeth out?" Dr. Pot took a step

over to the counter and glanced down at the open file folder that contained Darla's chart.

"In October," Darla said. It was now May. That was part of why she hadn't come in for her six month cleaning—paying for the wisdom teeth. Three had had to be pulled, or so everyone kept saying for years and years. They had all been impacted.

The one non-impacted tooth, the one that actually bothered her by growing jaggedly into the side of her mouth, had been easy to pull with a local anesthesia weeks after her first son was born. She had been more afraid of the wisdom tooth extraction than of the birth, though it turned out the birth definitely took much longer and involved more pain. The rest of her wisdom teeth, the impacted three, were clearly a different story. They didn't bother Darla at all, but their presence had inspired all the dental professionals she had seen for the last ten years to make dire predictions about how they would eventually disorder the entire contents of her mouth. Maybe aging was like that, though she had thought aging was supposed to happen much, much later. In her mind she felt she was still growing up, but had to admit coldly to herself that at thirty-five, she really wasn't. "You need to take care of yourself," her older female sisters had begun to urge in frightening tones, and so she agreed to get the final three impacted wisdom teeth out.

"Go under," Dr. Pot's entire staff had said, as had Dr. Pot herself. The periodondist's staff concurred; general anesthesia was worth every penny. "Otherwise, you'll hear your bones cracking," the periodondist's assistant had said during that preliminary visit to find out just how bad things were.

Hours and hours after her initial consult with the periodontist, after preschool was over and board games played and fights had turned into melees and dinner made and eaten and cleaned up and the boys bathed and then finally asleep, the movie her husband rented didn't pan out because it was too slow. In the darkened TV room, they ate popcorn and Darla told Tom about her dental situation. Tom casually wondered aloud about the price and necessity of general anesthesia while drinking a microbrew that cost three dollars a bottle.

"It's going to cost sixteen hundred dollars to have them out with the general," said Darla. "The general part is six hundred."

Tom pretended to choke on his popcorn. "Do you really think you'll need it? I'll bet they can give you lots of Novocaine and a bunch of other stuff for pain. You know how dentists are. They'll take you for every penny."

Years ago, before the boys were born, when Tom was twenty-four and they lived in New Mexico, a dentist from the Northeast Heights had used fancy video equipment to convince Tom his gums were about to slip off his teeth. It was going to cost thousands of dollars to reverse the damage. Darla forced him to see her dentist, a kind man with an unpretentious office on the outskirts of downtown Albuquerque, close to their apartment. Her dentist assured Tom that all he needed was regular brushing and a small cavity filled. Darla knew Tom's present insensitivity was a result of that bad experience, and of having had only three small cavities his whole life. Her fillings could set off airport security.

Having morphed into parents with Tom (they had gotten together originally in college, before either of them had even been twenty) made her feel oddly competitive with him, as if he were another son she had to fend off in any number of rambunctious ways, or a brother with whom she was constantly jostling for attention or rights. Having kids sometimes made her feel like a kid: at best, joyful and carefree and wild, and at worst, petulant, petty, and whining. She and Tom were no longer primarily lovers, though they still made love and sometimes it was hot and heavy and great. Things had changed. With kids they had become a family, and as Darla knew, families were complicated, and got in the way of good sex.

Her own parents had what they called "bad teeth." Despite that fact, they allowed her and her siblings to drink gallons of Kool-Aid each week. (Darla's boys were allowed two small glasses of 100% fruit juice each day, and after that milk or water.) Many times she had made the Kool-Aid herself, leveling off cup after cup of grainy white sugar, pouring it on top of the Kool-Aid dust dumped at the bottom of a plastic pitcher. She had to turn her head away from the fumes when she turned on the tap and stirred in the water. Now when she saw Kool-Aid on the shelves in the grocery store (she was shocked it was still available, still legal), it made her think of the Jim Jones incident that happened in South America when she was a kid.

Darla hadn't wanted to interrupt the dental conversation and distract Tom with her Jim Jones recollections, though she felt guilty insisting on general anesthesia when she remembered that kids as well as adults died during that mass suicide. Talking about money was difficult and depressing enough. They used to have a sufficient amount. It was great that they both had flexible schedules, lots of time with the boys, and were both *going for their dreams*, but it was costing them a pretty penny, and the lack of benefits sucked.

"I wish I didn't, but I *need* the general," she told Tom as they sat on the couch in front of the blank television. She chomped popcorn and tried to avoid using the two five-year-old porcelain crowns on her left rear molars. "I'm going under no matter what." The crowns had cost six hundred dollars each and she wondered if they had a shelf-life. They were almost as old as her oldest son.

She had cracked her molars chewing ice when she was pregnant with him. In pubs, while others drank their pints, she stupidly chewed ice in an attempt to stave off cravings for a dark porter and a Marlboro Light.

Darla took a couple of unpopped kernels out of her mouth and threw them back into the silver bowl after thinking about where else to put them and not liking the idea of putting them (all spitty) on the floor. Tom made a grossed out face, put the bowl of popcorn down, and slugged the rest of his beer.

"Okay," he said. "Do it. Go under. Not a problem."

"Ka ching, ka ching." Darla pretended to ring up a sale. She felt she had to acknowledge their growing debt, that wild unsavory fungus.

"Don't worry about the money! Do what you need to do!" Tom grabbed the remote and switched the television on to a public television station where an old man was describing how economic downturns lead to spiritual development.

"I'm tired," said Darla. "Let's go to bed." She had known that night that she would take a long time flossing.

In the cubicle, Dr. Pot dropped the tooth-color samples onto the counter on top of Darla's chart and picked up the metal instruments again. Darla opened her mouth. Her gums were sore from Matt's thorough cleaning. Dr. Pot seemed to be poking around more brusquely than necessary. She tapped Darla's bottom row where her front two teeth slightly overlapped.

"Hard to clean," said Dr. Pot. "Does it bother you, the way it looks?"

Was it just her imagination, or was dentistry beginning to have an exclusively cosmetic emphasis? Next they were going to ask if she wanted liposuction on her puffy gums, or to reconstruct her tongue to make it sexier. If Doctor Pot suggested one of those torturous daytime retainers, Darla was going to smack her.

"Just tell me if I have a cavity, okay?"

That seemed to shut Dr. Pot up, or at least refocused her attention.

"The x-rays look good," she murmured, her hands moving inside Darla's mouth. "Maybe when you are working you can do the other things for yourself."

Or maybe I'll just walk around with crooked yellow teeth and pretend to be British, thought Darla. Hello—she *was* working. She painted in every spare non-exhausted moment, was employed half-time doing the books for a chiropractor, and the rest of the time she worked plenty hard raising her children while her husband Tom wheeled-and-dealed nonstop to build his client base. They were both making money, just not *enough*. Darla let herself return to a previous worry. Had the wisdom teeth been some sort of scam after all? Dr. Pot wore a small gold cross around her neck. Did she attend some kind of church? For some reason, Darla had a hard time trusting people who were extremely religious.

The periodondist who had taken her three impacted wisdom teeth out had been a born-again Christian. Darla figured that out when he smiled approvingly at his conclusion that she was a stay-at-home mom (her boys came with her for the preliminary consult; she couldn't find a babysitter). He told her his wife used to be a teacher, but was now home-schooling their kids so they got the *right values*. Darla immediately stopped fantasizing about being married to him. He was much too brutal and doltish looking, with his crew cut, khaki pants, white socks, and boat shoes, anyway. She had been only momentarily swayed by his beautifully tanned, muscled arms, and his probable buckets of money. Tom had an innate, understated, intense sexuality that she imagined would grip her indefinitely. Right now, he just had no money. Of course she could be making more money, too, but there were the kids to take care of, and she was trying to keep painting, even if it wasn't really going anywhere (*right now*, she reminded herself, not going anywhere *right now*). If a job was too intense or serious or full time, she and Tom would have to fig-ure out more childcare for the boys, and even though most people wouldn't see the straight line starting at a full time job and two kids and pointing to the end of her painting life, Darla could see the arrow bold and definite, a sharp point at its end: the painting would go away, would evaporate silently like water in a dish.

Dr. Pot hummed quietly as she checked each of Darla's teeth for decay. Darla had to admit that Dr. Pot was very thorough, though the cynical part of her brain interpreted Dr. Pot's thoroughness as a way to dig out potential problems, or even unloose a perfectly fine old filling. Perhaps she was getting paranoid; she decided not to tell Dr. Pot about the tooth that hurt. She had had teeth hurt before and then stop hurting—sometimes the sensitivity simply passed. The exact opposite could also happen: after her teeth were crowned (and before the triple wisdom tooth extraction), she had felt deep pain beneath one of the crowns that wouldn't go away, even after she augmented many tablets of ibuprofen with lots of whisky and a little ice. The root canal cost a fortune and took two lengthy visits. Darla paid her babysitter well (a photographer friend she loved and trusted, and who needed the money) and used her "painting time" for the appointments, as she had done for the crowns months earlier. The root canal had not been painful, but it took forever, and it was tiring to keep her mouth open for two hours at a clip, even with the rubber block propping it wide.

"Hmm," said Dr. Pot, about to make her prediction.

"Dr. Pot," said Matt, the hygienist, coming back into the cubicle. "You have a phone call."

"What phone call," Dr. Pot said. "Take a message!"

"It's the school," Matt said. "Your daughter An."

"Please excuse me," said Dr. Pot, stepping out of the cubicle.

"I hope it's nothing serious." Darla put her hand over the paper bib around her neck. She knew it had spots of water and maybe even spit on it. "I didn't know she had a daughter."

"Yeah," said Matt. He removed the bib from around Darla's neck and threw it into the garbage. It was hard to tell what sort of expression was on his face. He was probably going to be cleaning someone else's teeth in just a few minutes, making that person laugh, too, so that she had to stop and catch her breath. "Two of them, actually."

"Really?" said Darla. "She looks so young."

"Single mom," said Matt.

"Divorce?" asked Darla, wondering about the cross around Dr. Pot's neck.

"Widow," said Matt, turning away, maybe because Dr. Pot reentered the cubicle, or maybe because he was about to laugh.

"Sorry about the interruption," said Dr. Pot brusquely, picking up Darla's chart and making some notes.

"Is your daughter okay?" Darla wondered if the girls with the crazy retainers at her son's school were Dr. Pot's unfortunate daughters.

"Stomachache. Stress, I think. Big math exam."

Exam? "How old are your girls?" Maybe Dr. Pot would think she was getting too personal. "I have two boys."

"High school. I told her: take the test, then I'll come pick you up. I'll use my lunch break."

"That sounds fair." Darla tried to imagine her two little boys in high school. Would they do wacky things to their hair, or wear baggy pants that sagged so low that their underwear showed? That style would change by then.

"Hard to know what is fair," said Dr. Pot. "You have no cavities, no significant decay."

"Thank you," said Darla. She couldn't believe it. Maybe Dr. Pot was just too distracted to find any problems with her mouth. "I hope your daughter feels better."

"What about your kids? You bring them here for a check up yet?"

"I decided on a pediatric dentist," said Darla.

Dr. Pot smiled tersely and left the cubicle. Matt was already gone. Hopefully Dr. Pot wasn't insulted that she hadn't brought the boys. The super-friendly pediatric dentist, with all her stuffed animals and computer generated "healthy teeth award" certificates might be giving the kids the wrong message, that dentistry was fun. Darla stood up from the chair and stretched. Maybe before clients arrived tomorrow the chiropractor would give her a free adjustment.

"Come right this way." The receptionist appeared outside the cubicle, reached in, picked Darla's chart up, and flipped through it. Together they walked to the appointment counter. Darla noticed the receptionist wearing a light blue version of her own suede sneakers. She felt mortified. The receptionist looked nineteen and had four different colors streaked through her hair, each in various stages of growing out. While she consulted her computer screen, Darla stood on the other side of the counter and tried, ridiculously. to hide her feet.

"Okay: cleaning, x-rays, exams. One hundred and eighty dollars."

Darla wondered with one part of her brain if she should write a check and just pay for it, in effect cleaning out their checking account, or if she should use a credit card and add to the shadowy mountain of debt that they were accruing each month at a steady and expensive rate. Another part of her brain wondered if tonight she would be spared that other weird dream she sometimes had, where her mouth was a giant cave, and she was some kind of explorer poking and hacking at her own teeth, searching for (or getting rid of?) something that would save her.

"Can I pay half by check and half on my credit card?"

"Sure," said the receptionist. "Too bad you don't have insurance."

Darla fought the urge to correct the receptionist, to tell her that she had medical insurance, just not dental.

Instead she said, "Actually, can I pay half today, and can you bill me for the other half?"

"Sure," said the receptionist so easily that Darla wished she had asked for a reduced fee or a freebie. She wrote the check and left the office. It was May, and still raining, but not too badly. The cool rain felt good on her hot face. Now she could pay the babysitter, the photographer who had a photo in a group show this weekend. Maybe she and Tom could go and take the boys for a little while. She had nothing to wear to an opening but her sneakers, but what else would she wear in this weather? She had a pair of cords that fit just perfectly and a denim jacket that would do.

When she got home, she would pay her friend quickly and tell her they'd see her at her opening. The boys were always anxious for her attention after they had a sitter. She knew they would want to play dentist. They would plead with her to open her mouth.

"What's that?" they would ask, touching her fillings. "Why do you have so many? Dad doesn't have so many, he just has three."

"Kool-Aid," she'd tell them, but they didn't know about Kool-Aid. "Make sure you brush your teeth."

"We know, we know," they'd drone and then ask, "Does this hurt? Does this?" The metal fillings always excited them, made them squeal and poke hard at each tooth. Darla would try to relax and just go with it for a few minutes.

Her older son would tell the little one, "Go find the shot," and the little one would run off laughing and look for the doctor's kit they got last Christmas. Darla would sit on the futon couch in front of the blank TV while her older son would say soothingly, "It's okay, Mom, it won't hurt," a silly grin plastered all over his lovely mouth.

His two baby front bottom teeth had recently fallen out, with lots of blood and screaming. The new adult teeth coming in behind the gap were broad. They didn't look like they could possibly fit, but (during a fifty dollar visit) the friendly pediatric dentist assured Darla they would, that the jaw would grow and widen, and the new teeth would fit perfectly. A month had passed, and it looked like the pediatric dentist was right.

When her little guy ran back into the TV room with the plastic syringe, both boys would nearly collapse from glee. "Time for your shot! Time for your shot!" They'd make her open wide and press the plastic syringe onto her teeth while they sang, "Almost done, almost done." They liked it best when she pretended to cry, the louder the better, so they could rub her back and pat her arm and tell her that she would feel better really, really soon.

# EXHIBIT

AMANDA WAS INTO PERFORMANCE, into getting off the page, but the words of her poems remained glued to the paper. She couldn't memorize them.

There was no place to sit in the living room. David's gear was spread out over the cushions of the couch—tomorrow morning he was going on a fishing trip. And at midnight, Amanda's mother was arriving at the Albuquerque International Airport. But first there was a poetry reading.

"You're not coming?" Amanda asked.

David was crouching in front of the couch, untangling fishing line, stretching his hand for the hook. "I can deal with poetry," he said, speaking to Amanda over his shoulder. "And I can deal with naked women. But poetry at a strip club?"

"All this equipment," Amanda wanted to say, "but no bucket." Instead she said, "I'm meeting Tanya at the reading. After it's over, she's driving me to the airport to pick up my mom."

"Sounds good." David was sorting lures into piles by weight. "Keep your clothes on."

Amanda left the apartment and started walking. Her favorite jeans fit snugly. So did her vintage satin blouse. The cloth-covered buttons looked like tiny pillows. Under her clothes she wore her only pair of black lace underpants, and a matching bra that made her breasts itch. She walked in the dark to the rhythm of her mumbled poems. Now all the words were in her brain, but onstage was always another matter.

Downtown Albuquerque had only three bars when Amanda had moved there from New York two years before, to be a copy editor at the newspaper. Albuquerque was a desert, but everything was growing: microbreweries, cafés, comic book shops, restaurants, and movie rental stores. When she met David, he was renting *Ferris Bueller's Day Off*. He was so handsome she decided not to worry about the implications. But though Amanda failed to memorize her poems, she could recall word for word a phone conversation she had had with her mother six months ago, the night David moved in.

"What's this guy all about?" Her mother was calling from Long Island, from the house Amanda grew up in.

Exhibit 77

"He's concerned about the planet," Amanda had said carefully as she watered her jade plant, omitting the things she actually liked about David: the flat muscles in his stomach, the zesty songs he made up in the shower, their fun sex in a chair with metal arms. The jade's soil was so dry she had to add water gradually, waiting impatiently as it soaked into the dirt.

"Concerned about the planet how?" Amanda's mother sounded suspicious.

Amanda answered her mother's question with a list.

"He's a vegetarian,

he's into alternative energy

and sustainable agriculture

and zero population growth."

"What?" her mother had asked. "He doesn't like kids?"

A dead brown leaf had fallen off the jade as Amanda shrugged, even though her mother couldn't possibly have seen the gesture over the phone.

Now her mother was in the air, probably flying over the Midwest. Probably zooming toward Wyoming or Colorado. And tomorrow morning David was leaving with his brother to fish. He never kept what he caught, though. Catch and release was his motto.

In the neighborhood Amanda walked through, yards were filled with wildflowers instead of lawns. The white flowers glowed in the streetlight. Large birds screamed from the nearby Albuquerque Zoo. They also screeched in the early morning, and sometimes the calls and cries woke Amanda from a dream, or became part of one.

The poetry slams Amanda read at were usually held in the bar next door to the strip club. Though she had read many poems and drunk many pints at those slams, she had never won. She feared her poems were too simple. Mostly she wrote about people and places and feelings. Occasionally she wove in a Greek myth. Some of the lines of her poems stretched to the edge of the page, as if she wanted to tell a story but didn't know how. Back in high school she wrote skinny floral poems about lust and inebriation, but that was a long time ago, long before she met David.

She had never been inside the strip club. David always pretended to go in when they walked by, and Amanda always pretended to steer him away from the door, though in fact she was interested in seeing women who weren't afraid to be naked in front of an audience.

As she neared the club, she still hadn't decided whether she would try to perform her poems from memory, or whether she should read them off the pages folded into the back pocket of her jeans, like she usually did. The poets who recited their work kept the audience riveted. Reciting from memory seemed straightforward, but each time Amanda tried, even the titles of her poems stepped out of her brain.

She opened the strip club door. Inside, a beautiful

EXHIBIT 79

bald woman sat on a stool. Her leather jacket looked like it weighed at least fifty pounds.

"Ten dollars." The woman extended her small white hand.

Amanda considered telling the woman that she was a *featured poet*, not an audience member, but the reading was a benefit for a safe-sex non-profit. So she just handed over a twenty and waited while the woman made change.

DISAPPOINTINGLY FEW PEOPLE were in the club. Behind a small bar, the bartender rubbed glasses. A few baffled men wandered across the dance floor in front of a low stage. The readings at the bar next door were always packed with rowdy college students and artsy twenty-two year olds—but then, there wasn't usually a cover. People weren't used to paying for poetry.

As she stood there looking for Tanya, Amanda felt like she was back on Long Island at one of the many sweet sixteen parties she had attended. It was the mirrors, the purple walls. At least there were no balloons or streamers. "Like a Virgin" wasn't blaring. She remembered the outfit she wore to one such party: a cardigan sweater, backwards, baggy corduroys, a long string of fake pearls. She could not find a bra with a low enough back and so she went to the party without one. She thought she would have to sneak out of the house, but her mother hadn't noticed her braless state. No one at the sweet sixteen noticed either, but Amanda could not stop thinking about her breasts the entire party. How old she would have to be before that memory and many others like it would cease to be embarrassing she did not know. She was currently twenty-five. By the time her mother turned twenty-five, she was married, owned a house, and had three children.

Maybe people didn't go to strip clubs on Sunday nights, or maybe, like David, people didn't care to mix poetry with breasts. Amanda felt flat-chested already. In a way it was a relief that David hadn't wanted to come. It would have been awkward, pretending not to notice as he pretended not to ogle naked women, though so far she hadn't seen any. Perhaps this was a poetry-only event.

She ordered a scotch and soda. Later, she'd have a drink with her mother in the living room after the flight, and it was better to stick with one type of liquor.

Tanya walked into the club then, wearing a sheer, long-sleeved black shirt so tight it looked like a wetsuit. "Well?" she said as she grabbed Amanda's glass, took a long sip, and made a face. Tanya saw herself as a spoken-word goddess, and said her poems about cats, wine, and broken wings were burned into her brain almost the moment they came to her. "I barely write them down!" she once confided.

Exhibit                                        81

Amanda pulled her poems from the back pocket of her jeans. The pages were creased into boxes. "Should I try to recite?" She felt pathetic, as if about to ask whether she could copy Tanya's homework. "Or should I just read them?"

"Don't should on yourself," Tanya said—though she no longer attended AA meetings, she employed many of the platitudes. She moved a couple of feet so that the lights hanging above the bar illuminated her chest. She was braless, her shirt see-through. "What do you think?"

"Tanya!" Amanda immediately regretted sounding shocked.

"Remind me where we are?" Tanya made an open-handed gesture that encompassed the mirrors, bar, stage and dance floor.

One-word lines began coming to Amanda, reminiscent of her high-school style:

I
can
see
your
boobs
I
can
see
your

boobs

I

can

see

your

boobs!

She wondered about breaking the poem into three separate stanzas. Maybe remove the exclamation point? Tanya's round breasts were slightly smashed by the bodysuit.

"Of course recite your poems," Tanya said, gesturing to an imaginary audience while using her hands to showcase her breasts, as if she were a model at a trade show convention drawing attention to a wonderful product known as her boobs. Several men in the club were in fact looking at her, elbowing each other and nodding.

Tanya was the only woman Amanda had ever met who actively loved her body. The friends in middle school who took their shirts off when they rode bikes at night later became bulimics, and the college roommate who danced topless at every party had recently undergone breast reduction surgery.

Glenn, the safe-sex reading organizer, walked toward Tanya. His denim shirt was more unbuttoned than usual, though his greasy blonde hair looked the same. Behind his back they called him Kurt Cocaine.

"Three poems each, tops." Glen glared at Tanya a mo-

Exhibit                                        83

ment; she had a reputation in the open-mike community for going over the time limit. Then his eyes moved
to her chest, where they remained.

"What do you think?" Tanya turned sideways to offer
her profile. "Am I making things harder for your imagination or just making things harder in general?"

"Nice shirt." Glenn grinned as he jumped up onto the
small stage. There was no microphone. "Welcome to the
benefit!" he yelled. "Sex is good! Sex is positive! It's all
about being safe!"

Tanya rolled her eyes and took another swig of Amanda's scotch and soda.

Amanda didn't see any of the local poets she had as-
sumed would be at the reading: not the small girl in
the blue beret who had a reputation for sleeping with
the other poets, not the guy with the Roman haircut
whose poem about the Victoria's Secret catalogue had
won him the slam on three different occasions, not even
the Vietnam Vet with the broken teeth and the poems
about Nietzsche. The audience consisted of disoriented
men—right club, but no naked girls—and Amanda felt
bewildered as well. How she had missed the clues that
this event was going to suck, she didn't know. Her only
comfort was that Tanya had missed them, too.

Onstage, Glenn was reading his poem:

> "White tile bright light
> sink as hard as my dick..."

Tanya mimed a finger down her throat. Amanda ordered another drink. Eventually the woman in the poem would bang her head on the sink and blood would drip onto the tiled floor. The sad truth was that when Glenn got up on stage Amanda knew each and every word of his poems. When he finished the sink poem he began reciting the one about his motorcycle. She wondered how old Glenn was, and at what point reading poetry in bars, or worse, strip clubs, became uncool. Glenn looked at least thirty-five. When Amanda's mother turned thirty-five, there had been a big party on the back porch. Amanda had been twelve; in a strange coincidence, she had gotten her period for the first time on her mother's birthday. Her mother had cried and hugged her. When the party was over, fireflies were blinking in the backyard, and her mother stood and chucked the ice from her drink into the grass. Amanda loved her mother's body, her wordless gesture, the careless way she flicked her wrist and ditched the ice.

Tanya was elbowing Amanda, reaching for another sip of scotch.

"And now, sexy poetess Tanya McCurdy." Glen said before he jumped down off the stage.

"Right on," Tanya whispered, warming up her sexy poetess voice. She stepped up onstage and turned to face the audience. Through her shirt her breasts gleamed like illuminated grapefruits. Someone ripped a wolf whistle.

Exhibit                    85

A man with a droopy handlebar mustache began to stomp. Amanda looked at her watch. Soon they were due at the airport to pick up her mother. When Tanya began her second poem, Amanda finished her second scotch. Her brain felt syrupy, and looking around, she thought about how she had never seen her mother naked. Not once. She thought of a modern dance performance she had seen in college: the dancer alone onstage, dancing without music, wearing nothing but a pair of shorts, her hair cut like a little boy's.

She nervously fingered the buttons on her vintage blouse. She couldn't concentrate on Tanya's poems; soon it would be her turn to read. The urge to pee was overwhelming.

At first the strip club bathroom looked like any bar bathroom: condom dispenser and no paper towels. Then Amanda saw the hooks on the wall, where fishnet stockings, garters, bustiers and baby doll nightgowns were hanging. Black satin, white lace, green gauzy stuff, leopard prints. On a shelf bolted into the cement wall sat several wig-topped foam heads and a cardboard box, the word "pasties" written in lopsided script. The wigs were a study in contrasts: geometric black bob, long blond shag, cascading red curls. The bald woman who worked the door was leaning toward the mirror, plucking her eyebrows.

"I thought this was the bathroom," Amanda said. "Sorry."

"It is the bathroom; it's our dressing room too. What can I tell you?" The bald woman blew a hair off the tweezers. "It's a low rent place. But poetry?" She leaned close to the mirror again and Amanda thought she might be arching her back just a little bit, showing off her bum in black leggings. "Now that's a weird gig."

"I know," said Amanda. She entered a stall, slid the latch in place, and peed. David had said he would clean up the living room. He said he would wait up to meet her mother, said he would have the scotch and soda and mixed nuts ready. He wouldn't be able to stay up *too* late. He wanted lots of energy to stand in the river, catch a fish, unhook it, and throw it back into the water, where it would swim away only to be caught again by someone else. Perhaps Amanda was alone in thinking there was something unkind and exhausting about this series of activities.

She flushed the toilet and washed her hands at the sink. The bald woman was still at the mirror. "You're not hot in that jacket?"

"I'm hot," said the woman, "under my jacket."

"Ha ha." Amanda waved her hands in the air to dry them. "Why are you here?" she asked, even though she already knew.

"I'm a dancer," said the woman. "But I'm not really working until later. You're one of the poets?"

Exhibit                                              87

"Yeah."

The woman grimaced. "I could never get up in front of people like that."

Are you kidding? Amanda wanted to say. Instead she asked, "What happened to your hair?"

"That's a really personal question," said the woman. "And I'm actually a very private person."

"Sorry," said Amanda.

"Cancer," said the woman. "Not now," she added, after registering Amanda's shock. "I got better and it grew back, but I discovered I like it this way. Now I have it shaved. Might as well, right? I call it Beyond-Brazilian. I have everything else waxed. I like wigs. Make-up, too. I like that feeling—erasing and creating myself, you know?" She unzipped one of the many pockets of her jacket and offered Amanda a metal tube.

Amanda read the small circular label on the bottom of the lipstick: "Fire and Ice."

The woman was back at it with her tweezers. There must have been one tiny hair she just couldn't remove. "Check it out. Try it on. That red is so fifties, right? Just like mom. It kills them every time."


WHEN AMANDA EMERGED from the bathroom, Tanya was standing next to Glenn at the bar, waving. "Here she is, Glenn! Here she is! Nice lipstick!"

"Where the fuck were you?" Glenn muttered, then hopped up on stage. "Our last poet tonight: Amanda

Jones." His voice was flat. So she wasn't sexy, fine. She wasn't a "poetess" either.

The stage lights made it hard to see the audience, though Amanda knew the men were out there. Their silence felt impatient. She left her poems in her pocket and let her hand slide down the V of her blouse. She could feel that the men wanted to watch, plump button by plump button, until the blouse was open, then shrugged to the floor. She licked her painted lips.

> Zoo Animals
> The stork
> banged his giant beak
> on the hard packed dirt
> zoo life confused or depressed him
> was there something essential
> about being a bird?
> If so, he'd forgotten.

A short film ran through Amanda's brain. When she was a child and took a bath, her mother told her to "clean between her legs." She had learned the word vagina from a book, mistaking it at first for the southern state.

> David
> Fishing
> in the river

Exhibit                          89

catch
and release
I will break up
with him
before he
can break up
with me


She had thought that men knew who they were, but now that she was standing in front of them, she could feel their confusion. Her need to keep speaking was internal, insistent.


The Story
Of mother
brains and bodies
what we know
how we know it
who we are
what we tell
what we remember
what we forget


Beneath the hot lights, Amanda refused to absorb the men's disappointment: she wasn't taking off her clothes. Unconcerned by the lack of applause, she stepped off the stage.

# INVISIBLE

CHLOE UNLOCKED HER apartment door and pushed it open. She didn't want to go home but there was nowhere else for her to go.

"Isn't it funny," said her roommate Donna, sandpaper momentarily still and silent in her hand, "that you moved from Long Island into the city to act, but that you keep getting acting gigs on Long Island and not in the city?"

Chloe tried to act like she thought Donna's observation was funny. All it took was a small chuckle and woefully shrugged shoulders.

Donna returned her attention to Operation Desert Storm. She liked to watch TV while she sanded. Tonight she was removing chipped paint off an old rocking chair.

When Chloe was tired, Donna's Nordic wool sweater and uncomplicated artisan's face were irritating. Still, Donna was a valuable roommate: she paid her share of the bills on time, did her share of the dishes, and didn't invite men to sleep over. Donna said she was bisexual, but Chloe had never seen her with a woman, either.

In the bathroom, Chloe undressed, took her red flannel pajamas off the hook, and put them on. She pushed her feet into white fuzzy slippers and shuffled to the kitchenette where she filled a bowl with potato chips, opened two bottles of beer, put everything on a tray, and shuffled back to the living room. She had to tell Donna about Brian. Though it wasn't clear how it had happened, Donna was the person she talked to the most.

The call from Brian's twin brother Lou had come this morning, at her crappy data-entry day job, before *The Sound of Music* rehearsal, a million hours ago. In a quiet version of Brian's rowdy voice, Lou informed her that Brian was dead.

"How fun! A party!" Donna sat back on her heels, took a long slug of beer, crunched a few potato chips, and resumed sanding. Two nights ago when she pulled the rocking chair from a heap of Park Slope garbage and dragged it up three flights of stairs to the apartment, the rocker looked like a hunk of junk.

Chloe had witnessed these transformations many times in the last eight months. Donna salvaged bookcases, coffee tables, end tables, and chairs. She sanded the furniture, painted it, and hauled it to a nearby elementary school whose gym turned into a flea market on Saturdays.

"If I paint it a really cool paisley, do you think I can get two hundred dollars for it?" Donna made her living this way, though she had majored in English. Aside from the actual labor of finding the discarded furniture, sanding it down, and painting wild designs on it, Donna's chosen path seemed effortless. It was strange how her square carpenter's hands didn't match the rest of her delicate body.

"You always get your price," said Chloe. Donna didn't have to go on humiliating audition after humiliating audition to get an unpaid acting gig. She never had to worry about rent or groceries and she didn't seem to care about clothes. (When they were first roommates, Chloe asked Donna if she ever wanted to show her work in a gallery. Donna laughed.

"It's furniture," she said. "Not art."

"It's beautiful," Chloe insisted, because it was true and because it was difficult living with someone who wasn't aspiring and failing.)

Chloe opened her mouth to tell Donna that Brian was dead, but Donna was starting to sing. "*The hills are alive with the sound of music…*"

"Please stop."

"What do you think?" Donna gestured toward the television. "Have we watched too many war movies to be moved by actual war?"

Chloe didn't answer. Donna liked to pose provocative questions, behaving as if she wasn't interested in normal conversations. Often Chloe found herself riled up by Donna's questions. Tonight she decided to act partially deaf.

Maybe she should wait to tell Donna about Brian; it seemed very possible that the military had gotten it wrong, anyway. So far the war had seemed so easy. Maybe Lou misunderstood; maybe Brian wasn't dead. Even though she had waited all day to sob and tell someone about Brian, now that Chloe finally had a chance, what she really wanted to say to Donna was something negative about the rocking chair.

"I'm cold," she said instead. She was tired of sitting on the living room floor because they didn't have any furniture. Except for the television, the living room was empty.

Donna threw a blanket across the room and continued sanding. She had knitted the blanket with exceedingly soft wool, but it was even more beautiful to look at than to feel. A word popped into Chloe's head when she first saw the blanket: *love*. The blanket was pink and orange, somehow mod and retro simultaneously. But color, style, and yarn couldn't explain how Donna had knitted such a wonderful blanket, and Donna didn't appear to know the value of what she had created. The evening she finished knitting it, she left it in a heap on the floor of the living room, went garbage picking, and returned home an hour later with her current project: the rocking chair.

"Are you going to sell this too?" Chloe asked, lifting a corner of the blanket and swishing it gently across her cheek.

Donna smiled tightly and nodded. "Of course."

When they moved into the apartment a year ago after recently graduating college (Chloe from the SUNY Purchase drama program, Donna with a degree in English from Cornell), Chloe thought Donna would furnish the apartment with her creations, but Donna sold everything she made and the apartment remained empty. Material possessions and appearances did not seem to interest Donna. Sometimes she wore the same pair of maroon sweat pants and blue oxford shirt for an entire week.

The war was still on, but it was hard to see what was happening due to the terrible reception. It would clear up if they got cable, but they had agreed they didn't watch enough TV to merit the expense. It was like the furniture; they didn't want to spend the money. Chloe didn't *have* any money after paying for rent, food, utilities, and clothing, and it was clear that Donna was the type who saved rather than spent. Without cable the war appeared yellow, then acid green. Streaks of light flashed across what looked like a hazy sky and low white buildings seemed to be exploding. Bombs may have been whistling through the air; it sounded something like that. Then it sounded like the crackle of a radio, like they were overhearing army commands.

"Compared to watching *Born On the Fourth of July* or *Full Metal Jacket*, watching Desert Storm on television is like watching a fucking laser light show," said Donna. It typically took her a very short time to become indignant when she watched TV.

Chloe couldn't think of a witty or politically correct response. She was uncomfortable lying on the bare wood floor, but the weight of her fatigue was becoming even heavier under the warmth of Donna's blanket.

When Congress authorized force a week ago, Donna wanted Chloe to go with her to the United Nations to march through the streets, to protest the war. Chloe said no. Donna went anyway, even though she knew Brian was over there on a ship. Donna said she liked Brian, though she also said that she would never in a million years sleep with a man in the fucking military.

Donna had her ideals; she was raised in rural China by missionary parents.

Chloe was the only child of two Long Island endocrinologists. She knew these facts about their childhoods implied hardship on one side and ease on the other, but what Donna didn't know was that Chloe's parents had perused her body for signs of abnormal growth. Donna didn't know that Chloe's earliest memory was of her father chasing her through the house with a measuring tape. ("He was playing a *game*, he wasn't *chasing* you, for God's sake." Her mother's version.) Donna didn't know that when Chloe turned eleven, when her breasts were just beginning to push up, when her hips just beginning to push out, her mother sat at the dining room table each morning with an invisible clipboard, pencil, and questionnaire.

"Did your period come last night?" Her mother asked as if she couldn't care less. "Any pubic hair or hair growing under your armpits?"

"I'm not a patient!" Chole insisted. "You can't study me!" That didn't mean she didn't study herself in her bedroom mirror, turning her naked body side to side to see new swells and curves. Her breasts grew bigger and her waist looked tiny.

Donna didn't know how lucky she was that her parents were too busy subsistence farming to micromanage her every move. Donna didn't know anything about the stupid brutality of typical teenage American life. It was actually *impossible* to watch a laser light show on television. A laser light show wasn't the Yule Log or Desert Storm. A laser light show had its own ritual. You got stoned in the parking lot of the train station, then took the train to the planetarium with your stoned friends, and listened to Pink Floyd while the fake dark sky filled with colored light.

"Voila," said Donna and popped the last potato chip in her mouth. The rocking chair was completely sanded.

Chloe shuffled back into the kitchen for more chips. The Operation Desert Storm portion of the news was over; it was time for local murders.

"Sorry if I was insensitive!" Donna called from the living room. "You must be worried about Brian!"

"Of course I'm worried about Brian!" Chloe heard her voice ring through the apartment. Without furniture or rugs there was nothing to absorb the sound; it went bouncing down the hallway. Donna didn't say anything more. Chloe worried that she had unwittingly warped back into her role as Maria in *The Sound of Music*, and had actually sung that line: *Of course I'm worried about Brian!*

She dumped the remaining potato chips in the bowl and knew she would not tell Donna about Lou's call. Brian just didn't feel dead. How could he be dead when she could shut her eyes and see him leaning over the railing of an immense aircraft carrier, flicking the butt of his cigarette into the salty water? Anyway, if she told Donna about the phone call from Lou, Donna would be forced by roommate etiquette to comfort her, even though inside Donna would be thinking: Navy-boy

Brian fucking got what he signed up for; he fucking got what he deserved. Donna might even be relieved by the thought of no more visits from Brian on leave, no more ecstatic moans in the night coming from fucking big-mouthed Brian. Chloe always tried to shut him up, but her efforts were in vain. When Brian had an orgasm, he practically yodeled. He was acting, obviously. No one could be that loud. He was overacting. He didn't take himself, or sex, or anything that seriously. That was the best thing about Brian. His lack of seriousness delighted her, even though she suspected he was spoofing her, especially spoofing her job: acting. Only occasionally did she wonder if she should enjoy being ridiculed.

There was only one beer left in the refrigerator. Chloe poured it into two short glasses. She would continue to imagine Brian's ship cutting forcefully through the waters of the Persian Gulf and forget about the other scenes she'd imagined, the ones of the aircraft carrier getting bombed and blowing up. She had never been with a soldier before Brian. Before Brian she went out with other actors, or musicians, who were definitely one hundred times worse than any soldier could be, no matter what Donna thought. It was true that Brian had said some distasteful things, like, *We're just going to blast the shit out of the Iraqis and not even get our hands dirty*. Unfortunately, Donna heard that comment. What Chloe loved about Brian was that he never stood her up, never

On Saturday morning, when Donna was at the flea market, Chloe called Brian's twin brother Lou. She sat on the living room floor with the phone and looked at the blank TV. Nothing but cartoons Saturday mornings; she hated cartoons. She wished she could cuddle up in the blanket and rock, but Donna had taken the chair and blanket to the flea market. Maybe they wouldn't sell. Right. People went to the flea market just for Donna's stuff. Lou wasn't home, so Chloe left a message.

"Hi, Lou. It's Chloe, Brian's girlfriend. Please call me when you can." She left her number very slowly, articulating each digit distinctly so that Lou would not be able to pretend he couldn't hear the message.

Brian had often talked about his twin. Lou was a New York City firefighter. One night when Brian was on leave, the three of them had plans to meet at a Moroccan restaurant, but Lou didn't show. Brian said that while they were at the gym together in Howard Beach earlier that afternoon, they had argued about weightlifting. Howard Beach was where they had grown up, where Lou still lived. After their parents died in a car crash when they were teenagers, Lou was Brian's only family.

"How can you argue about weightlifting?" Chloe had asked. Siblings were so mysterious. She was sitting cross-legged on cushions next to Brian at the low table in the Moroccan restaurant. Brian didn't answer, but he laughed. His eyes were on the line of belly dancers slinking into the dining room one by one. He rubbed a hand back and forth across his crew cut and pulled his wallet from his back pocket. Brian tipped big and Chloe didn't mind. She liked watching the belly dancers, too. They were not the thin girls one expected to be on display in Manhattan. They must be acting; they couldn't possibly be at peace with all that jiggling flesh. Some of them were even old. If Chloe's mother were here, she'd be noticing the dark mustache above one girl's lip. Her father would be pointing out the constellation of moles on an older woman's back or muttering about scoliosis.

Brian had one arm draped around Chloe's neck and was rhythmically squeezing her shoulder. In his other hand, he waved a five dollar bill. The dancers chimed their finger cymbals wildly and sashayed toward him. All the other men in the restaurant reached for their wallets.

"Me and Lou fight about all kinds of shit." Brian laughed and smiled up at the belly dancer closest to him. He tucked the five dollar bill into the skirt hanging from her hip. "Lou's an asshole," said Brian fondly. Chloe didn't get it; as an only child, she had no frame of reference.

Their appetizer arrived—the Moroccan pastry filled with ground lamb, dusted with powdered sugar, and drizzled with honey. The chubby dancers made Chloe feel free. She took several huge bites of pastry and forgot about Lou. She leaned against Brian's muscular chest and watched, mesmerized, as the fat around the dancers' bellies and hips swirled and rolled with the music.

LOU CALLED BACK Sunday night. Chloe had taken the pillow from her bed and was resting on the wood floor of the living room after a dress rehearsal of *The Sound of Music*. She was watching *Murder, She Wrote*, though static and wavy lines were making the episode impossible to follow. Donna was out, searching for treasures in the trash heaped like small mountains on the sidewalks of Park Slope. Tomorrow the garbage men would come and take it all away.

"Hello." The voice on the phone sounded like Brian's without the constant undercurrent of a joke. "This is Lou, returning Chloe's call."

"Why did you and Brian fight about weightlifting that time we were going to get Moroccan food?" said Chloe. "How stupid was that?"

"I don't remember," said Lou.

"Weightlifting," said Chloe. She laughed bitterly, skittering into high drama. "Do I finally get to meet you now, now that Brian is supposedly dead?"

"Brian told me you were an actress." Lou cleared his throat. "I'm pretty upset too. Brian being dead isn't a theory. They gave me his dog tags."

If Lou wanted to believe that Brian was dead, that the military had its shit together enough to get every detail right, that was his problem. Here was a man who fought about weightlifting.

"You're choosing to believe that your last family member is gone?"

"It's not a *choice*." Lou's voice caught on the last word. He took a breath and continued. "Look, Brian told me *you're* an only child. He told me you hate your parents. So you're alone now too, right?"

"Your parents are dead, so you don't have to hate them, right?"

Lou emitted a short laugh, or cough. "I can't believe you just said that. Do you want to tell me where to meet you, or should I hang up the phone?"

"I'll tell you where to meet me," said Chloe, and gave him the address of the coffee shop across the street from her day job. For many hours she sat in her cubicle entering data about the sale of fruit. Lou said he would meet her Wednesday, late afternoon.

"I'm hanging up now," said Lou, "before you can say anything else completely stupid." Chloe was glad he couldn't see the water leaking out of her eyes. She realized she should call him right back. She needed to change the day; she couldn't meet him Wednesday, just hours before her first *Sound of Music* performance out on Long Island. She was punching his number into the phone when the apartment door swung open and Donna began dragging metal chairs into the living room.

"Check these out!" Her voice was full of joy. "Eight chairs and two small tables." The paint was peeling and the vinyl seats were torn, but the chairs were adorable, their metal backs twisted into hearts. "From an old ice cream shop going out of business. Can you believe it? I'm definitely looking at a thousand dollars."

Chloe mustered all her professional training in order to act extremely excited about the metal furniture.

At work on Wednesday afternoon, Chloe stood in one of the cubicles blessed with both a window and an absent employee, and watched as Lou arrived at the coffee shop across the street. Instead of songs from *The Sound of Music*, "I Feel Pretty" from *West Side Story* kept running through her head. She told herself to quit it, to stop feeling excited, to get into a somber state of mind, but her body wasn't listening. It was hard not to feel the way she usually felt when Brian was coming home on leave. Her blood rushed faster than usual, her body hummed with anticipation. *So pretty and witty and gay!* And like idiotic background vocals, she heard Brian having an orgasm: oh-oH-OH louder and more ridiculous with every moan.

Chloe took the elevator down. Inside the coffee shop, Lou was drinking an espresso. He still wore his fire fighter's duds: stiff canvas pants and jacket. When he saw her walking towards his table, he stood up, and everyone in pinstripes and pumps stared at Chloe with envy. A second espresso sat across from him on the table. When Chloe sat down she noticed that Donna's metal chairs were exactly like the ones in this shop. So were the tables. Donna was right; she would easily get a thousand dollars once she painted everything and redid the vinyl.

"For me?" she asked, gesturing toward the espresso. Lou nodded and she took a sip. "Thanks." Lou had Brian's almond shaped eyes, the same crew cut, same jaw, same dimple, same almost-cleft in his chin. This made it hard not to feel as though she were acting in movie, or existing in a dream world, an alternate pot-and-Pink Floyd-induced reality where Brian was playing some kind of trick on her; it made it hard not to feel that maybe Brian wasn't so sexually straightforward, that maybe this was just his version of dressing her up as a French maid. Because she was transported it was extremely difficult not to grab Lou's hand, not to lean over the table, not to kiss him, French style, with a fair amount of tongue. *Act paralyzed*, she told herself so she wouldn't actually do any of these things. *Just act.*

"Well?" said Lou. "Do you want to talk about Brian?" Lou was brawny and robust, but beyond that he didn't look good. Shadows ringed his eyes and his shoulders slumped as if too much weight had been heaped upon them.

While he looked at her, while he waited for her to speak, she tightened her leg muscles and pressed her feet against the floor, pulling her metal chair tighter to the table, her knees further under it. Her knees bumped against his. Electricity jolted up her spine.

"What I want to ask you about is tonight," said Chloe. "I'm an actress. I want you to come to my performance. Will you come? The show's out on Long Island," she added apologetically.

"What's the address?" Lou sighed like a man who lived in a world that gave him very little choice.

SINGING THE FINALE at center stage, Chloe saw Donna in her orchestra seat and on the opposite side of the theater, Lou sat in his. It hadn't been hard to reserve a ticket for him and leave it waiting at Will Call; the show wasn't sold out. Lou was wearing a charcoal sports jacket, a white shirt, and a light blue tie. Donna had taken the Long Island Railroad from Brooklyn, then a cab from the station to the theater in Huntington. Chloe had made sure to leave detailed directions for Donna. She had no idea how Lou got here from Howard Beach.

Donna's blonde hair was spread over her shoulders; she never wore it that way in the apartment. From the stage it looked like an aura circled her head: she looked like she was glowing. It was amazing how much Chloe could see and think about while she was acting. During the performance she had watched the faces of Lou and Donna go from sunny, as Maria romped with the Von Trapp children, to cloudy, as the story switched to Nazis and World War II. It wasn't just Lou and Donna, the whole audience was with her. She saw it on their foreheads and lips, then heard it in their clapping when the show ended.

Chloe hurried to the lobby as fast as she could after the curtain, but she was too late to prevent Donna from running into Lou, whom she must have been surprised to see, and then become even more surprised when she found out Lou wasn't Brian, but Lou.

Donna cradled a big bundle wrapped in brown paper. It was tied with a string. Donna and Lou were almost the same height, but Donna was svelte and feminine in an embroidered Chinese dress, her hair still shining like silk over her shoulders. Lou was well-muscled, male. When Chloe stepped toward them in the lobby, still wearing her stage makeup and costume from the final scene, they both looked over and she could see the very same emotion as it flickered across each of their very different faces. Before the emotion vanished, Donna thrust out the package she held in her arms.

"Here," she said. "For you. You didn't tell me about Brian." Her voice was bewildered and sad.

"What is it?" The weight of the package registered in Chloe's arms, and she knew without removing the paper that Donna was giving her the blanket.

SEVERAL HOURS LATER, in Howard Beach, Lou was snoring, but Chloe was awake. Lou's bedroom was entirely without light. No glowing clock radio sat on the night table. Thick shades did not permit even one moonbeam to penetrate. In such darkness Chloe couldn't breathe. Better to stand, pull on the clothing she could find by groping, and walk into Lou's small living room. The blinds were up and the lamps from the street filled the room with dusky light. When her eyes adjusted, she could see everything in the room, not the specifics, but their dark outlines. Brian's navy photo was tacked above the stereo. She had seen it immediately when she entered the apartment, but turned quickly away to throw Donna's blanket onto Lou's couch and follow Lou into his bedroom.

Now she stood in front of Brian's picture, swaying unsteadily with hunger and fatigue. Brian wouldn't speak to her. Not a word. She looked out the window. The street was quiet. The houses were small, either brick or covered in aluminum siding. Howard Beach seemed like such a weird place for a single, well-paid man to have an apartment.

In Lou's refrigerator Chloe was surprised to find a

muffin wrapped in plastic. She poked around until she found some tea and made a cup. She sat on the couch with her tea and muffin. The couch faced the photograph of Brian. She couldn't actually see Brian's face unless she turned a light on, but then the light would be visible under Lou's bedroom door, and she didn't want him to wake up. She already knew what Brian looked like. He was undeniably handsome. So was Lou.

Half an hour ago she was in Lou's bed: his skull growing huge, his mouth transforming into a tooth-filled trap. When he finally shut his eyes, she shut her eyes too. He climbed her like she was a mountain. The sheets fell off the bed. The pillows smashed against the headboard. The hair on Lou's arms matted under her sweaty hands. When he was ready and he thought she was ready, he began fitting himself into the place she could actually see as a small separate room in her body. At that moment, she took the opportunity to go into another small separate room where Brian wasn't dead.

The tea was cold now, but Chloe finished it. She couldn't remember eating the muffin, but it was gone too. The worst part had been Lou's disappointing silence. He didn't say anything when he made love. He barely made a noise. There was a weird disjointed feeling too, a not-in-sync-ness. Chloe knew what it was like, what sex with Lou was like, but now she couldn't call Donna and tell her, though Donna was the one she wanted to call and tell. The word that described sex with Lou was *jarring*. Sex with Lou was like stubbing a toe. His snores reached into the living room, stopping and starting without any satisfying pattern. Chloe looked at Brian's photograph above the stereo.

"Listen," she said out loud to Brian as she pulled Donna's blanket up to cover her shoulders, to keep herself warm. "I'm going to keep faking it with your brother." Chloe saw how it would have to be. She would evolve a whole new school of invisible acting. The stage was one thing; you needed to be big on stage. The screen was another; you had to get small for the screen. But the bed was something else. Her strategy would be successful because Lou knew she was an actress. Subconsciously he would expect her to act. He wouldn't be able to see or feel or smell her technique, the work would be so deep.

# MOON

LUCY REMEMBERED (or maybe she dreamed it) life before Celia was born. Gulls circled overhead while she stood on wet sand. A giant triangle of pizza dripped from her hands. Her parents swam. Gulls screamed and swooped down with the sunset. The pizza flew off in a beak. Lucy ran. In the waves she grabbed her mother's long hard legs. Her father lifted her, and held her against his wet torso.

O

LUCY WAS NINE, Celia, seven. Lucy was City Girl and Celia, Country. They played City Girl Country Girl on roller skates in a parking lot.

Country Girl had long straight hair pulled into a

ponytail. She knew ponds, cabins, camping. Ate corn on the cob cooked over fire pits. Her boyfriend wore boots, called her Sweetheart, sniffed her green-apple hair. Country girl was never lonely, never chubby, never sad. Mom and Dad gave money for hay rides, lip balm, pale t-shirts, white bikini underwear that never stained.

City Girl was a delicate, store-bought flower. Her hair never frizzed, her skin never pimpled, her white teeth had no food stuck in them. Her boyfriend wore Musk for Men, called her Babe. She was never lonely, never jealous, never sad. Mom and Dad were opera singers who drowned on an ocean liner that sank. They left behind lots of money for high heeled sandals.

Celia skated forward, then backwards through the parking lot. Lucy called out scenarios, guidelines, relationships. Celia opened her legs in a *plie* and skated down the center line of the parking lot, sideways. She did it again, faster. Lucy joined her, made Celia take her waist. Lucy skated hard, Celia hanging on, bumping over broken blacktop, screaming. They skated home for dinner. Lucy double dared Celia to skate ten yards with her in the busy street, but Celia pretended not to hear, and skated on the sidewalk. She grasped the street sign as she rounded the corner, used her momentum to beat Lucy home.

O

CELIA GOT her breasts first, too, when she was ten and Lucy, twelve. Lucy had a box of pads and a bra waiting in her closet. From the bathroom Celia called out Mom! Mom! like she'd seen the devil in the mirror instead of her own round face. Lucy heard her mother say Congratulations! (She stood beside the bathroom door and listened.) Her mother's head popped out. Go get that box of pads for Celia! Lucy went to her closet, lifted the pink box. A beautiful girl ran through a meadow. Lucy had already opened the box. Just to hold one. Just to sort of try one on. She handed the box through the bathroom door and walked to a deserted schoolyard to sit in a swing.

O

LUCY AND CELIA walked the long driveway. In the backyard their relatives sat in a lawn chair circle. Babies ran in soggy diapers gnawing plastic teething rings.

Lucy went around the circle, kissing cheeks. She leaned over and kissed her uncle's friend on the lips by mistake when he moved at the wrong moment; she kissed a strange man. He didn't seem to mind. His wife sat next to him. Lucy's back hurt like it always did. She tried to straighten up. The man's young wife raised her eyebrows.

Celia was standing next to a bucket filled with ice. Come on, she said, and held up two cans. In the front yard, slugging black cherry soda, Celia hooted. You got him on the lips! On the lips!

O

ON THE PLAYGROUND one Friday during recess, Celia sat in a circle of seventh grade girls, painting her nails the colors of sour balls. Bitterness, like fungus, sprang up in the girls overnight. Hate circulated through bloodstreams. They didn't like Celia anymore. They told her that. Celia crawled out from under the slide, spilling blue glitter polish on sand. She ran laps around the infield field while the girls lay on their backs, yelling at the sun to give them a tan.

O

IN THE PARKING LOT of the mall, Celia's foot landed on a naked woman, legs spread, breasts large, nipples dark. She put the photo in her pocket and found the mall bathroom next to the deserted frozen yogurt shop. In the bathroom stall she looked at the photo and peed. One of the woman's hands was in her mouth, the other between her legs. The woman looked straight at the camera. Celia felt accused by her, by this tiny woman. She flushed her down the toilet. A month later, she found a picture of a man with his penis sticking straight out; it jabbed at her, made her need to catch her breath.

O

BY THE TIME she was fourteen, Lucy was no longer able to see her own body accurately. It appeared alive only when she looked at it in the mirror. The mirror became a type of frame, but only for her face. Her hips didn't fit, her thighs didn't fit, her ass didn't fit. She was not a glossy, bone-thin girl, not a chilly martini to drink off the page. Her real life was blubbery. It wasn't super-color-saturated. It didn't have a cool grainy finish.

O

MANY YEARS LATER a long black bug clings to the screen of Lucy's window. It is an unfamiliar end-of-winter bug, spawned of slush and two days of sun. Lucy feels too fleshy. The hair on her face and body has darkened all winter.

Stay right there, says her lover, right there where the sun is streaming through the windows. Take your clothes off slowly so I can watch you do it. He's in bed like a soap opera star, hairy chest above the clean white sheet. Yes his eyes are heavy-lidded. Yes he is breathing through his mouth.

Lucy does not want to remove her clothes. If she takes them off so he can see her, she knows she will not get wet. For when she noticed the hair on her upper lip was getting darker, she also noted fat protruding over the elastic of her underwear. And her thighs seemed flabbier. And a pimple popped out on her ass.

Lucy has to feel good about her body to get aroused. How she can feel good about her body when her body is both a picture in her mind and a creature with its own wild life. Her body won't be tamed no matter what she does to it.

The bug on the screen stayed all day, complete as a jewel, warming itself in the sun, because with that tiny brain, it didn't know how to do anything else.

O

SOME YEARS LATER Celia met Robert, fell in love with him, and got married.

Lucy was two years older. She should have gotten married first. She didn't mind too much, since Robert, Celia's husband, was so completely not her kind of man. Except when he smiled a certain way, and his lower limp crumpled.

O

CELIA FELT PANGS at odd times—not when seeing a baby in a carriage and so forth. The pangs had nothing at all to do with babies. They began inside her belly. Her belly was changing, just like her face had changed after college: cheekbones higher, face bereft of a certain charming softness. Her periods, previously so heavy and healthy feeling, inspiring her to run around the block ten times or beat somebody up at least once, slowed to a trickle. She began to cramp, to note how many days she bled. She began to fear that it was time and possibility, the merging and multiplying of cells, slipping away instead of plain old blood. Celia began to forget to put in her diaphragm when she had sex with her husband.

On the other side of town, Lucy's period arrived along with ravenous hunger. Each cookie she pushed into her mouth tasted better than the one before it. In her shiny magazine she read about "how to satisfy your man in bed" and "the new small belt." Lucy decided against the skinny belt. And she already knew how to satisfy her man in bed when there was one. The cookie package rattled empty. She gave herself permission to seethe. Everything about men made her crazy. Their breath, their hair, their simple clothes, the stupidity of their desire, the reluctance of their giving, their dim sense of justice, their shallow scope of sarcasm, their lack of zest.

Lucy cried at commercials, took hot baths lit by candles, consoled herself with fresh ideas for work and wardrobe.

O

When Celia was six months pregnant, she fit herself into the closet in her bedroom, the closet she shared with her husband. She shut the door and pulled the chain to get some light. Only half these shoes fit her feet. Her worst suspicion confirmed itself in how she hated to see her clothes on hangers next to his clothes, how she hated for her shoes to be mingling with his shoes. He was out there, in the bed that was half his. It was terrible to hear him call, Celia, what are you doing in there? It took all the energy she had to open her mouth and say, nothing, to pull the string and stand in the dark.

That morning Celia woke up to her husband's hand on her breast, his fingers in her pubic hair. His fingers circled, her sleep receded, and Celia grew wet. Her husband's hand found her nipple, pulled it softly, rubbed it lightly with its open palm. Celia wanted to bite something. Soon his hard dick was up against her butt, pushed between her legs, trailed in between her thighs. Celia imagined him watching where he placed it. He was fascinated. Was she repulsed, exhausted, or deeply aroused?

O

Lucy and Celia wallpapered the baby's room. The roundness of Celia shocked both of them. (Lucy's own weird pregnancy never registered, years ago, the terrible cramps and gelatinous bleeding, how she soaked tampon after tampon and finally just sat on the toilet to bleed. Is this normal, she wondered, but never asked. Pregnancy had not crossed her mind.) Celia measured and cut wallpaper. The windows and doors were all open. Lucy was on and off a chair. Wet paper was dripping. To Lucy, Celia looked contemplative, scary. Lucy stared at her while she matched the still dry roll next to the paper that already hung on the wall. Why are you looking at me? I'm not, said Lucy. I'm fat! Celia accused. She eyed Lucy's flat stomach. You're beautiful! You're gorgeous! Lucy grabbed the next wet piece of wallpaper and climbed back onto the chair. Celia stood behind her, eyed the pattern, directed. The sticky sponge in Lucy's left hand pushed out the wrinkles in the paper and her right hand matched the seam. One of the seams refused to come together. Lucy finally lifted the paper from the wall to reposition it. A chunk came off in her hand. Lucy screamed and held up the piece she ripped. Celia took it, slapped it into place. There, she said. Get the rest of this done before it dries funny.

O

IT WASN'T a vacation. It was Celia's business trip. Celia brought Lucy to share the hotel room for fun, since she was seven months pregnant and couldn't have any. Lucy was thirsty, poured more wine into her glass. This finished the bottle. I have another bottle, said Celia. She wanted *someone* to drink. Not yet, said Lucy. The hotel room spun. In what seemed like less than two minutes to Celia, who was lying on her side across the hotel double, big belly bulging, Lucy said, where's the wine? I want more wine. Celia was so sleepy. The bed was good. Watching Lucy get drunk was fun. Wine, more wine, said Lucy. She opened another bottle. When she turned back to Celia, Celia was snoring into a pillow. Lucy watched her pregnant little sister sleep.

Because Celia was sleeping, Lucy flipped through a magazine. She didn't think she was looking for meaning in the pages that regurgitate plucked eyebrows and hip huggers. *Oh it's fun!* She was just flipping through a magazine. But she absorbed their complicated messages, then fell asleep and dreamed.

On the other side of the double bed, in her sleep, Celia's loneliness became a lump she could not swallow, like peanut butter stuck in her throat. She became reluctant to speak for fear that words would betray her.

O

THE SISTERS each had this dream and thought it was her own.

A deposit of dead things not yet decomposed was trapped inside her. Rotten apples, broken branches, egg-shells, coffee grinds, and dead leaves heating up.

At last she pushed her hand down into her body and pulled out puzzle pieces, the legs of dolls, odd socks. She pushed her hand deeper, uncovered a half-rotted log, a marble, a cigar box. It hurt to pull them out, especially the box. Inside the box was a green pencil with her name on it, printed in gold lettering. She stood on the earth and turned all the way around to see the objects hanging from limbs of trees where they flew (she threw them): green pencil balanced in a branch, odd socks draped over dead flowers. She debated breaking the surface of the earth, but decided she was too tired. So she wrapped her arms around the heaving animal heavy dead alive scratching thing within her and rocked it.

# VISITING PHILLY

**1**

THE PANEL! Is there a way to honestly inform frolicking nineteen-year-olds about sobriety, marriage and motherhood without making life sound utterly disheartening? Hillary rings Camille's bell, but Camille doesn't come to the door. It's strange to be back in West Philly, near the dorm across from the frozen yogurt shop where they flirted with beefy frat boys and ate melon-berry yogurt for dinner. That was fifteen years ago. Tomorrow morning they'll return to U Penn as panelists on the alumna forum: *how women negotiate and navigate their lives*. Even in the new millennium, apparently, the women studies department eschews capital letters. The women-studiers must have contacted Camille first and

Camille must have insisted they invite Hillary. Her credentials (former art history major, part-time speech therapist, mother of twins) hardly make her a dazzling poster-woman for limitless feminist possibilities. Camille isn't home yet. Hillary sits down on the freezing condo steps to wait. *Panelist* is beginning to feel like *contestant*.

Today, with blow-dried hair and spit-free clothes, she could pass as a non-mom, but it's impossible to stop thinking about the girls: their meds, their occupational therapy, whether Leon will be able to handle it all until she gets back Sunday afternoon. She knows it's ridiculous, but she dreads Camille noticing how *prompt* she's become.

When they were students, *she* was the one who woke up late in strange rooms. Without knowing her exact location, she could safely assume the bed she was in belonged to a handsome male. The telltale signs: empty beer bottles, dirty ashtrays, Poly Sci textbooks, whiffs of aftershave and sweat, were all in evidence, as was the handsome male himself, sleeping open-mouthed beside her. Her head banged. She needed water. More time would pass before she could even lift her wrist to look at her watch. She was confident Camille was roaming the dorms, looking for her, searching the quarters of probable boys. Hillary listened for the knock at the door, for Camille to whisper, "Hill! Are you there?" Her cue to decamp.

In the almost-empty cafeteria they debriefed: Camille mod in black eyeliner, geometric prints, and pointy shoes, Hillary a typical ratty prep, frayed collar and cuffs, unraveled sweater, hem hanging loose from her plaid skirt. Hillary swallowed clunky tablets of ibuprofen and sipped black coffee while Camille ate a large bowl of Cap'n Crunch. A drop of milk clung to her upper lip. Several oranges rolled on her tray. Picky about boys, Camille had little to report; she was, however, unfailingly eager to interrogate.

"What happened last night?"

Hillary held up a finger: not yet. She had to concentrate on pushing the pain out of her head. When the last section of orange disappeared into Camille's mouth, Hillary bummed a cig, knocking her ash into the peels.

"You know Jim G. right?" There were too many Jims at U Penn. "We went back to his room, and he put on Earth Wind and Fire, and we were fooling around, and he started begging: *touch it please touch it*."

Camille was aghast, delighted. "What did you do?"

"I touched it," said Hillary, "and then I passed out."

Now THEY ARE old enough to be role models. Hillary's ass is freezing. She stands and tries to see through the high windows of Camille's front door. The ornate metal knocker on the door is obviously from a specialty catalogue; Camille has good taste and the time to leaf through home decorating magazines. Hillary lets the knocker drop again and again just to hear the sound. Something must have come up for Camille: beautiful single women without children have the wherewithal to be spontaneous.

Hillary checks her phone, her metal band, the coverage so good it's impossible to fly out of range. Camille hasn't called, but Hillary refuses to let it upset her; she'll take a walk instead of waiting. It's strange to be alone, to walk without a stroller, to exist without one of the girls in her arms (Larissa chewing her shoulder, Natasha pulling her hair), their small bodies mooring her to the ground.

## 2

IN WINE BAR, Camille sits with two men. The small metal table topped with uneven mosaic makes the delicate glasses tilt. They are drinking a German Riesling Camille agreed to order and now deeply regrets, having completely forgotten that Riesling is sweet.

The day has been filled with lucrative trades, sour meetings, and odd memories. Take the two men. It was strange to run into Josh at the stock exchange and then have him call Gordon for drinks, but that's what happens when an old friend like Hill shows up. Life's timeline flaps loose: no one can predict what tomorrow will bring. Pour on the drama. It's this sappy wine. Tomorrow brings the women studies panel at nine o'clock in the morning.

Negotiating/navigating. Camille has her plan for tomorrow's event. She'll focus on A Career in Finance, avoiding questions regarding Relationships and Children. Most of these young women will be feminists of course, some of them will believe themselves lesbians as well, but whatever their current identity, they will study the panel of alumna like life-sized 3-D maps. Résumé? Income bracket? Marital status? Progeny? Hair? Clothes? Makeup? Shoes? Cosmetic surgery? They'll ask questions designed to sniff out the truth; U Penn has always been big on critical thinking.

The drink with Josh and Gordon is taking longer than she thought it would; she should be meeting Hill in West Philly this minute. Choosing Reading Terminal Market was a bad idea, too. It's noisy and crowded and bright and none of them can hope to look better than they did fifteen years ago. The warm brie on the glass plate is delectable, however, and Camille eats slice after slice. Gordon is, as usual, quiet, so she chats with gregarious Josh, but another part of her brain is bumbling along an increasingly familiar path. She never used to ruminate about love. She never used to wonder if love was something outside her realm of possibility. Why would it be? Why should it? She fell in love, but always with the wrong man: wrong simply because the man didn't love her. It happened the other way, too, repeatedly: always a very simple, very wrong equation.

She developed complicated theories, but unlike stocks and bonds, her mind could never make sense of love. Love involved urges and longing. Couldn't the same be said about money? She was good with money. The Riesling was doing this to her, making her normally clear thinking smudged and tacky. When, in the middle of an anecdote, Josh orders another bottle, she hasn't the heart to stop him; she's not listening to a word he says.

### 3

HILLARY WATCHES the trolley roll to a stop. She gets on, drops her coins into the box and looks out the window at the Schuylkill River. Years ago she biked across this bridge, after midnight, no helmet, no bike-light, pockets bulging with tips.

Once across the river, she hops off the trolley. She wants to walk, to really see the Philly she remembers: splotches of cobblestone, dark Rodin statues, pop art, tourists and tepid department store displays. The Reading Terminal Market is across the street. Inside, she knows, bread, fruit and fish are piled into pyramids.

Camille won't understand the situation with the twins; she hasn't seen them since they arrived in the states. They were only nine months old then, and weren't supposed to be doing anything. Not like now, when they *should* be walking and talking. Not like now, when it's clear the girls have *special needs*.

Hillary's cell phone rings. A tremendous flock of pigeons startles the air. They careen around the corner of a building. She wonders if birds always know where they're going.

"Looking for me? I'm at the Market!" Camille often laughs on the phone, like the medium itself is a joke. She's sipping something. "Long story; I'm here with old friends." Another laugh. Maybe the friends don't like being called old. "Remember Reading Terminal Market? Come meet me!"

"Pick a spot," says Hillary, thrilled at the coincidence and irritated by the presence of other friends. She wants to ask, *Do I know these people?* But they're probably not *that* old. It doesn't matter; it's great. She'll show up in three minutes instead of thirty and shock Camille the way she used to back in college. "Tell me where you are." The Market doors are heavy enough to feel historic.

"Wine Bar," says Camille.

"Which wine bar? What's it called?" Hillary has entered the Market on the Amish side. The Amish women are in their caps, selling cookies and live chickens.

"Just *Wine Bar*," says Camille.

Hillary detects a slight tone of urban irritation for the cow from the suburbs. "Right," she says, and clicks off.

She could chuck the phone into a plastic trash bin this instant. Life would be so much giddier without a phone.

## 4

AFTER THE QUICK hang up, Camille tries to call Hill again, but presses the wrong buttons. It's definitely the wine. Perhaps Wine Bar is not such a good idea, since Hill no longer drinks. This is what negotiating/navigating and seeing Hill, the very idea of seeing sober and steady married with children Hill, is doing to her. It's transforming her into a woman who allows her leg to touch the leg of her silent old friend Gordon repeatedly under the small metal table.

## 5

HILLARY CIRCLES the Market, spots Wine Bar from the vantage point of Bonomo's Specialty Meats, and buys a pound of bacon from the butcher as an alibi. Camille is sipping wine at a table with two men who look like Josh and Gordon, guys from college Hillary *knows*, unfortunately, in the biblical sense. She returns to the Amish section of the Market to buy a pretzel from a girl in a white cap. The girl's forehead is shiny and round. The twins will be her age, sixteen or so, in thirteen years. Will they ever be able to make change or read? The pretzel is warm and doughy. Hillary eats it all, buys a coffee cake and stashes it in her bag along with the bacon. Apparently she's shopping for breakfast tomorrow, momming it up though officially off-duty. Maybe it isn't Josh and Gordon. So many years have passed since she's seen those two. But Camille? Unmistakable. Absolutely striking. Camille may be the most beautiful woman in the entire city of Philadelphia. Hillary buys a dozen eggs.

"Do you like being Amish?"

The girl tugs a rubber band around the carton of eggs and pretends not to hear the question.

Fifteen years ago she and Camille schemed about the Amish girls. They knew those girls could not possibly be happy wearing bland old fashioned dresses and baking. She and Camille would foment their escape by slipping them copies of *Playgirl* and *Ms.* That was the summer the two of them remained in Philly instead of going home for summer break. It was the summer they learned to lie. They lied to the restaurant manager to get waitress jobs. They lied to their parents about their illegal sublet. They lied regularly to the men who flirted with them at the restaurant. They lied to doormen of clubs to avoid paying covers. They learned how to lie without speaking. They lied with their eyes. Their breasts lied constantly.

They told their parents and their employer that they were getting a phone; they always said they were working on getting a phone, but they had grown to love not getting calls, to not calling anyone, to the exquisite freedom of handing out fake numbers.

## 6

JOSH TRIES to ignore that Gordon is making the moves on Camille. He tries not to resent how in general women always say, "I want a man who can communicate," and then in reality go for whichever dumb schmuck presses up against them first. He's employing his usual hyper-verbal strategy with Camille. It works with lots of women, but not with her. It didn't work in college and it isn't working now. Nonetheless, he keeps talking as he sips his wine. Surprises in the bond market, inside investor jokes that Gordon, a roofer for Christ sake, as well as his oldest friend, would never in a million years get. Unfortunately, Gordon isn't really a simple blue collar peasant. The man owns a roofing empire. Another thing that Josh has noticed during his long bachelorhood is that women, though they deny it, are in fact turned on by money. Camille is laughing at Josh's jokes and joking back, but Josh can feel the vibe between her and Gordon. The table is small, but not so small that Gordon and Camille have to sit shoulder to shoulder, elbow to elbow: he can only imagine knee to knee. In fact, he'd leave right now if Hillary wasn't supposed to show up, and if the Riesling wasn't so expensively delicious. He wants to see Hillary, though suddenly he's a little embarrassed to have her find him drinking too early in the day, having failed to marry, produce offspring, or leave Philadelphia.

Hillary had been enormously uninhibited. He'd no sooner shut his door and her clothes would be off, knees wide as she sat on the side of his bed, smoking a cigarette. Hillary never talked during their quick sex; she left her cigarette smoldering on top of a Coke can.

Fifteen years later and still, whenever Josh sees an untucked preppy girl, he thinks of Hillary. She must be different now; she's got *twins*. Josh wants to see it. He wants to see the wild girl made tame. And then there's that very slim chance that she hasn't changed. Then Gordon can have Camille, take her, she's gorgeous, but *so what?* Hillary is the definition of old flame.

"Hey, Comrades." Here she is, voice dry and crackly, the same. But Hillary's not schleppy-preppy anymore; she's chic. Her bulging oversized bag is a zebra print. She's thin and bluntly brown haired, wearing all black. Only her eyes show strain. She sets a large cup of coffee down on their small table. The three of them stand to hug her.

"How did you get here so fast?" wonders Camille.

"Wine?" Josh remembers too late that Hillary is sober. She's hugging him last, and he hopes best.

"No thanks."

Her bones feel fragile, a surprise. He's been recalling a sinewy agility. They all sit down in the uncomfortable cast iron chairs. Hillary smiles in turn at each of them. She's sitting very close to Camille, holding and patting Camille's hand. Her eyes fill with tears and he doesn't really get it, but there's something so wonderful, so familiar about seeing Hillary cry. He's seen her do so many naked things. He remembers suddenly that she fucked Gordon that one time and the memory makes him want to belt Gordon in the face again right now.

"Drink up! I'm just in shock." Hillary's giant coffee cup dwarfs their wine glasses; she's really sobbing now.

## 7

HILLARY TRIES to smile at her old friends to assure them she's not tragically depressed. Should she try to explain that crying is a treat? That the twins, like "normal" children, cry so frequently that it stifles her inclination to do the same? Mothering is repetitive enough. Then there's marriage, for better and for worse, but doesn't Leon like her best when she's upbeat? It's been years since she cried; she used to cry when she was drunk.

Maybe that's why her old friends don't look rattled. Gordon pours himself more wine. Camille maneuvers brie onto bread, then into her mouth. Josh watches a couple make out on a bar stool. Both he and Gordon have lost some hair; Leon's is still thick, still wavy.

"Maybe it's too much," mutters Camille finally, draping her arm around Hillary's shoulders, "to see Josh and Gordon too. You just got here. I don't know what I was thinking."

"We ran into each other this afternoon," says Josh, "which we in fact never do, and Camille told me you were coming. We got a little carried away with the idea of a reunion. We heard about the panel tomorrow." Josh is smirking.

Hillary remembers that smirking was the number one reason for breaking up with Josh fifteen years ago.

"He called me," says Gordon, speaking for the first time, using his thumb to indicate Josh.

"I'm so happy to see you." Hillary includes all of them in her gesture, but it's Camille she's happy to see. Unlike so many of Hillary's mommy friends, Camille doesn't haul around a diaper bag; her singularity makes her *glow*. Hillary leans against Camille's perfume and wine-scented body. She sips her coffee; she will not allow the lusciously fruity Riesling to cause even a twinge.

"Let's go." Hillary stands up. The wine is actually causing a major twinge.

Camille and Josh and Gordon stand up immediately. Hillary knows they know that she had to *quit* drinking because she could never just *stop*.

"Is the Art Museum still open on Friday nights?"

"Why?" says Camille, buttoning her blazer. "Where are you parked? You got here so fast."

"At your house; I took the trolley and then walked." Her friends don't get it, but they laugh, even Gordon. "I wouldn't mind seeing some art." She can see them making a frightening list in their heads: she was an art history major, now she's a speech therapist, she's on the wagon, her kids are disabled. Her childless friends will do whatever she says.

"This is a huge bag to be toting around," says Josh, picking it up.

"Breakfast for tomorrow," says Hillary, and they all laugh again. For a moment, nobody moves. The market is growing empty. Only a few customers remain, casing the stalls for Friday night supper. The fans that whirl hot air down from the high ceiling stop spinning. In the sudden quiet the fruit monger across the way throws brown canvas over his piles of oranges, bananas, and pineapples. Gordon clears his throat and starts walking toward the door where Hillary entered. Chickens squawk as their cages are moved. The Amish are closing shop. Hillary wonders what the Amish girl will do tonight. Square dance? How solid is her fortitude? Does she have a secret source? Outside the Market, the sun is going down. The air is even colder than it was before.

**8**

CAMILLE HOLDS Hill's hand as they walk toward the bus stop. She wonders what Gordon is thinking, what Gordon *wants*. He's so quiet. She wants to talk to him, but it's obvious Hill needs her. Hill may not get drunk anymore, but there's still plenty of vicarious drama in which to partake: her sobbing fits, her troubled twins, her sexy tempestuous husband, her fight to stay sober, her struggle to maintain what she's called over the phone her "deep sense of self in the face of mothering."

Gordon is walking up ahead with Josh. Josh was always so suspicious back in college, so curious, so hopeful that she and Hillary were more than friends, that they were lovers. Josh just couldn't believe that their friendship alone could be as interesting, as intriguing, as compelling as all that.

**9**

GORDON MARCHES them onto the bus because this ramshackle crew won't get anywhere unless someone takes charge. He pays the fares and supervises a transfer to another bus. Then everyone agrees to walk the last few blocks to the museum. Josh is hefting Hillary's tote, good naturedly complaining of its weight. Camille and Hillary are walking together, holding hands. By their lowered voices and occasional laughter, Gordon assumes they are gossiping; he hopes not about him.

He hasn't had a day like this in what feels like forever. His days are usually so predictable, so evenly split between the South Philly offices of Perkins Roofing and his childhood home in Upper Darby. His father's been dying of lung cancer for months. And since his mother died two years ago, and his three younger brothers are all married, Gordon said he'd do it, he'd move back home to help his dad and supervise the hospice nurse. His brothers have been appreciative, but they can't know what it's like, trying to sleep each night, the burly old man dying one room over.

Gordon wants to unburden himself to these women he knew so well so many years ago, but now is not the time to describe watching his parents die, how it makes him really feel his own mortality. He won't go on and on about how he still has issues with his dad or how Perkins Roofing is a myopic world of materials and contracts essentially designed to repel the elements. He knows his thoughts are getting loopy and strange, so he keeps quiet. Plus Hillary seems on the verge of something big herself and they had a saying during a period of mushroom experimentation in college: one freak out a night, please.

Those two keep doubling over with laughter. When he looks back they're barely walking, they're laughing so hard. He and Josh are already a whole block ahead of them. He could talk to Josh, but that's not really their pattern. The pattern is Josh talks and Gordon listens. The other way around is uncomfortable. The truth is, Gordon much prefers talking to women.

He's not a complete dolt. Camille was definitely coming on to him in the bar. There's nothing, seriously nothing he'd like better than to spend the night with her, hell, the whole rest of his life with her if she wanted it, in her surely beautiful, sweet smelling home. He needs a break from himself and from his father's last gasps. He needs a break so badly he drank white wine tonight.

It's the time for a game plan, a scheme, but that's always been his problem. He can never think of one. Hillary and Camille must be far behind by now. He can't even see them anymore, but Camille knows where she's going. They'll meet on the steps of the Art Museum, the famous Rocky steps. The theme from the movie runs through Gordon's head. Josh is unusually quiet.

Gordon hates to think about what Josh might be remembering. Sleeping with Hillary that one time was stupid on a number of levels. Josh punched him, Camille got chilly, and Hillary pretended it never happened. The worst was the sex itself, a beery nothing that left him morose and ashamed.

It doesn't have to be tonight with Camille; he can call her. They can go out for a good meal or listen to some jazz. They're not in college anymore, they can't just fall into bed like idiots. Gordon looks up. A few stars twinkle in the Philly sky. Tonight is fine as a good omen, if that's all it ends up being. Plus you never can tell with women. Maybe his luck is finally turning.

**10**

HILLARY WALKS up Parkway Boulevard with Camille, ravenous for something rich, something French, something someone else has spent a long time preparing. Flags celebrating Philadelphia flap from poles in the wind. Gordon and Josh are no longer visible. They're probably already inside the Art Museum, getting warm in the lobby. Hillary has that all-laughed-out, all-cried-out feeling. Her face is ice. She won't let go of Camille's hand; she can't.

The small Rodin Museum en route to the Art Museum is squat and dimly lit. She wants to see the famous doors, The Gates of Hell, but it's too dark to really make out any of the twisting figures, so she runs her free hand over Rodin's cold metal and tries to remember what Hell looks like.

When Camille says something about Gordon, Hillary can't quite hear it. Josh has her tote, the food for breakfast, her phone, her notes for the women studies panel that begins in less than thirteen hours. She doesn't want to feed anyone, talk to anyone, help anyone else to advance. Those smart young women at U Penn are already so far ahead of the twins.

She veers off Parkway, tugging a tipsy Camille. Down the block is a bistro with a lit up sign. A sentence forms in Hillary's sober brain. A mother doesn't ditch her kids unless she really cracks. Inside the small restaurant, a server appears.

"Pinot noir," orders Hillary. She likes those particular words in her mouth, the way she gets to say "no" twice in a row. She's squeezing Camille's hand so hard now it must hurt.

"Nothing for me." Camille is staring. "What are we doing? What about Gordon and Josh? What about not drinking?"

"Men aren't children." The server returns with the wine. "Just one drink." Hillary shuts her eyes, her hand on the stem of her glass.

"Don't. Don't!"

Hillary opens her eyes, disappointed. Red wine spreads across the white tablecloth. She's never been a hoarder, but never before has she needed to hoard. Her daughters are going to take everything.

# HOT SPRINGS

## 1

FRIDAY NIGHT in the frozen food aisle, Jen grabbed cans of OJ and found room for them under the bread in her brimming cart. In her mind she replayed a dream from Thursday night: a sandy beach, leaning back on her towel, slowly peeling off her bathing suit, her breasts somehow glistening, a muscled young man watching. Waves of lust rose from her body. When the bathing suit was off, she looked at the man, at his face to say yes, but instead of a face there was a disappointing blank spot, then a black screen, a quick dream shift to another setting: her halter suit back on, tied tightly around the neck. Jen was swimming, it felt dangerous; she was swimming with her two children, in a round circle of too deep, too cold water.

Down the aisle, Jen saw Pamela Hoffman next to the desserts, reading labels on sorbet. If anyone or anything could make Jen feel guilty, it was running into a single mother (especially one made blamelessly single by widowhood) when Jen was busy resenting her children and husband: her *family*. Right now the word had a heavy weight.

In her plush red jogging suit, Pamela looked fit. Both Jen and Pamela were former New Yorkers and knew each other as parents—their children attended the same elementary school—as well as professionally. Jen was director of Albuquerque Community Gardens, Pamela, a master gardener. Both believed passionately in starting any project with the best possible soil. Neither enjoyed pointless chit-chat. Two weeks ago at a Garden fundraising event, Jen had "introduced" Pamela to Ralph, the handsome music teacher at their kids' school. Of course Pamela knew Ralph already, as Mr. Hill, music teacher, but she didn't *really* know him. But now she did. A mutual acquaintance had told Jen that Pamela and Ralph had apparently already gone out for coffee. Twice! Each time Jen thought about how she had introduced Pamela to Ralph, or envisioned them chatting over coffee, she got distracted. Curious. Distracted.

The bouncy new wave song on the supermarket radio was loud (Jen used to dance to that song every time she heard it, regardless of where she was) and the high pitched sound of a drill being drilled somewhere in the cavernous store was disorienting. Jen hated bumping into people at the supermarket; shopping was such a personal impersonal activity. Plus she was trying to remember her sexy and then suddenly un-sexy dream. Plus she didn't want to hear details about the coffee dates. Unhealthy varieties of pot pies tempted Jen in the giant freezer to her right, but a box of blueberry waffles already threatened to tumble down the slope of her groceries. Pamela was so engrossed in her label reading that Jen wondered if she could slip by her without an interaction. But Pamela looked up.

"Oh, hey Jen," she said, eyeing Jen's full cart. "Doing a big family shop?"

"Yeah," Jen said. "Hi, Pamela." Pamela's handheld basket contained three turnips and a clutch of beet greens. "How's it going?"

Pamela made her no-bullshit face and added the container of raspberry sorbet to her basket. "I've been better." Pamela's voice, her persistent Queens accent, always made Jen surprised that her nails weren't two inches long and dotted with rhinestones. (Although she wouldn't be able to garden that way.) "The kids are at my in-laws this weekend, so I'm a little lonely."

Jen wasn't jealous! But didn't divorced (and even widowed) people sometimes have an advantage? Just that sometimes people took their kids to give them a break, or the ex-spouse had the kids for the weekend and then they were free? Of course, Jen had babysitting lined up with her in-laws for tomorrow. She and Charlie were taking a day trip to the Jemez hot springs in lieu of their regular date night. So she wasn't complaining.

"I'm sorry to hear you're lonely," she said. (Though she actually found it hard to believe.) "What are you doing tomorrow?

"Just working in the yard," Pamela said. "Rock garden-in-progress."

"Charlie and I are going to Jemez hot springs," Jen said. "Want to come?"

Pamela laughed. "I'm sure Charlie would love to have me hemming in on your romantic date!"

"You know men," Jen said. "Two women are better than one."

Pamela laughed again, this time sounding slightly offended.

"That sounded horrible," Jen said. "Charlie's easy-going, that's all." He was. He never got pent up and put out the way Jen did. Charlie found life laughable.

"I don't think so, but thanks." Pamela looked down at the list in her hand. "I'd better get," she said. "I've got a few more things to pick up."

Why wasn't she out with Ralph at a movie or something? What was going on between them, anyway? "Wait!" Jen tried not to sound desperate. "I just had a really funny idea."

Ralph sat across from Jen and Pamela. Jen ate her *huevos rancheros* and took a good look at the men as they ate. In this proximity and morning light, she noticed with discomfort how much Charlie and Ralph looked alike. Both were tall and thin and in good shape: easy smiles, no beer guts, no bulbous noses, no hair sprouting from ears. Aside from fine wrinkles around their eyes (and to be honest, some thinning on top), the men could be twenty-five. Well, maybe thirty. Charlie was a runner and Ralph played hockey. He didn't look big enough, but apparently Ralph was tough; he'd been playing for years. Jen knew this because months ago she'd volunteered to play piano during the school's holiday recital and had to have a couple practices just with Ralph (on tuba) and they were talking about this and that and he told her he played hockey. Where's the rink? They were practicing in the school music room. Where do you find ice in Albuquerque? Jen's voice got girlish as she improvised a chord with one hand and played the melody with the other. She purposely smiled at Ralph. Why do you want to know? Ralph's voice was deep. He sounded slightly irritated. Do you skate? Do you want to skate? He punctuated this last question with a raunchy toot from his tuba. I could teach you. Jen kept playing the piano and didn't answer.

Even after the recital and holiday was over, Jen found she was thinking of Ralph, thinking, Ralph makes me smile, Ralph makes me laugh, though when she tried, she could never remember him ever telling a joke or even being funny. Charlie was the funny one; Charlie made her laugh all the time. What was wrong with her? What made her set Pamela up with Ralph? Was it because Pamela was a widow and Ralph was divorced? Was it because, since she obviously couldn't, she wanted someone to date him? Yes. It was because she was stupid.

Jen chewed her breakfast and tried not to wonder what Ralph looked like naked. Just like Charlie? It was ridiculous; if she was going to have a crush (and after the first uncomfortable confusion of it, Jen enjoyed it, enjoyed the feeling of interest and the new awareness of herself, and of Ralph and of Charlie, an awareness she hadn't realized she'd missed), why did she pick a man who could easily stand in for her husband, at least in photographs? It felt irritatingly Freudian, though her college memories of psychoanalytic specifics were dim. But Charlie was different. He wasn't musical, though he enjoyed the blues. Charlie was numerical, a very smart, successful CPA.

Charlie enjoyed eating his breakfast; he shoveled his *huevos* and chewed with gusto. Ralph blew on each forkful before putting it into his mouth. Pamela pulled off chunks of her tortilla and methodically dipped them into the pool of red chili on her plate. The silence made Jen want to smack someone.

"Garcia's has the best red chili in Albuquerque." Jen

hoped her bold statement would get the four of them arguing, talking. New Yorkers have their bagels, their cheesecake, their steak; New Mexicans have their chili.

"El Modelo's is much better," Charlie said flatly, taking a sip of coffee.

"The Sanitary Tortilla Factory is best, bar none," said Pamela.

Charlie shook his head. "Tourist trap."

"Lots of locals eat there!" Pamela said defensively. "Don't roll your eyes!" She leaned over the table and punched Charlie in the arm, then turned to Ralph. "What's your favorite?"

"That really hurt," Charlie said appreciatively, rubbing his arm. "You pack a wallop."

Why did Pamela need to touch her husband? Jen turned to Ralph. "What about you, Ralph? What's your favorite?"

"Hmm," Ralph said, smiling, nodding, mulling it over. "I don't limit myself to favorites." He looked Jen directly in the eye. He was still blowing on his chili before putting it into his mouth. It couldn't be that hot.

Jen blushed while Charlie continued to extol the virtues of El Modelo, its purity, the way the same working men lined up each day to get their lunches from a crew of silent, unsmiling women in hairnets. "Like a church," Charlie said. He was a faithful but austere romantic. "Plus, it's cheap." He grinned.

Ralph nodded, but didn't agree. "I guess I like to play the field," he said, looking first at Pamela and then at Jen. "What can I say?" He put another spoonful of chili in his mouth; you could eat it that way in New Mexico, like soup.

Charlie snorted and left the table to pay the bill at the counter.

Pamela laughed loudly. "Good to know, good to know," she said to Ralph and elbowed Jen in the ribs. Then she whispered in Jen's ear, "Is there something I should know about you and Ralph?"

"Don't be an idiot," Jen whispered back. Ralph was watching the two of them; he looked satisfied, almost smug. Jen resisted the urge to rub her side; Pamela's elbow really hurt. She was a master gardener: strong from digging holes, cutting back overgrown bushes, transplanting failing perennials, pulling tenacious weeds. She believed in xeriscaping, in using as little water as possible. She liked to do a lot with a little. "It's my credo," she often said in her unmodified Queens accent, "my motto, my challenge. What can I make out of nothing?"

Jen tried not to think that Pamela had perhaps tempted the fates with her boasts and bravado. (And caused her husband's death? Ridiculous!) Given Albuquerque's diminishing water supply, of course Jen, on a professional level, agreed with the philosophy and practice of xeriscaping, though sometimes she found herself dissatisfied by hardy high desert plants like agave and yearned for a lush pink garden full of greedy water lovers like foxglove and bleeding hearts.

When Charlie got back to the table, Pamela started talking about the fantastic *sopapillas* at the Sanitary Tortilla Factory, about delicious drizzles of honey. Jen sipped her water and allowed herself the beginning of a fantasy: Pamela falling ill suddenly (the chorizo?) and going home, and Jen going to the hot springs with Charlie and Ralph by herself: the three of them in one rocky pool. Jen had a vision: her rounded shoulders squeezed between their more muscular yet bony ones. The horrible truth was she wanted them both. Everything in her life at this moment was sharing, compromise, just how little she could get by on: time, money, attention, sleep. Back to the hot springs: they would have a truly paradisiacal feel, a warm yellow sun, glistening brown rocks, light green aspen leaves shaking in a turquoise sky.

Only rarely did Jen regret being married, the ring on her finger, the vows, the years that had produced a boy and a girl, one five, one six, both probably watching cartoons at Charlie's parents' house this very minute, cartoons with guns and nasty characters who shouted—the ones Jen forbade and the kids always begged to watch. If she was regretting her marriage now in Garcia's New Mexican Restaurant, it was only a little part of her doing it, a little leftover single part thrilled by wilderness:

old growth trees, black bears, trilliums, the part that found gardening—planning and planting, nurturing and cultivating—tedious and stifling.

## 3

No ONE SAID much in the minivan on the drive up to the hot springs, and this bothered Jen; she realized she had been counting on Pamela to keep some sort of interesting conversation going. After all, Pamela was a New Yorker. She liked to talk. But Pamela was looking out the window. Overall, Jen found that people living in Albuquerque didn't talk enough. That wasn't it, exactly. They didn't have intense opinions? They didn't fight? No one flipped the bird while driving. (Charlie had made her stop, said he was afraid he'd get beat up, she'd flip the bird and he'd get beat up.) Sometimes New Mexico felt so spread out and sunny, so uncomplicated. She wasn't stupid or naïve; she knew about gang-related drive-by shootings and even heard gunshots occasionally at the edge of their country club neighborhood, where they lived in a modest house with, of course, a big garden. She knew about land grants and grazing and water rights and sovereignty issues and about the seemingly basic distrust the three ethnic groups, Hispanic, Native, and white, nursed for each other. None of it was personal for Jen; she found the dusty New Mexican conflicts ultimately alienating, because (though she was white) none of it was about her. Except for the water, maybe—the way the water, the giant aquifer beneath Albuquerque, was being drained by overuse. That was something that troubled her, that she couldn't ignore, and she earmarked a sizeable portion of the Community Garden budget for water conservation education.

About halfway to the hot springs, Jen remembered: music! She pushed in Bob Marley's greatest hits and in the passenger seat next to her, Charlie lit up a pretend joint with a pretend lighter.

"You don't really have pot, do you?" Pamela asked from the back seat, her tone either disapproving or disappointed.

"This is so fun," Jen murmured, trying to see in the rearview mirror just how close to each other Pamela and Ralph now sat.

"I happen to be prepared," Ralph said in a cheesy announcer's voice, waving something small in his hand.

Pamela gasped. "A pipe! Tell me you have marijuana!"

"I have marijuana," Ralph said.

The minivan zoomed smoothly through Jemez Pueblo. Little kids dressed in uniforms fanned out across the baseball field adjacent to the state highway. A kid popped a fly. Another kid caught it. A cry went up and the outfielders began running infield.

"Let's not talk about T-ball," Pamela said. "Or kids." By coincidence, all their children were on teams in the same league. No one responded to her request, but Jen thought about her children, the way her daughter crouched at the tee like a slugger and then missed the ball completely, the way her son searched for ants in center field.

In the rearview mirror, Jen watched Ralph use two hands: one to hold the pipe to his lips, the other to get the pot lit with a lighter. The autumnal smell filled the minivan and Jen felt a surge of lust. Charlie's sinewy legs looked good in the passenger seat beside her and Jen snuck small peeks in the mirror as Ralph (lungs full, making no sound, only gestures) offered the pipe to Pamela, who smiled deeply through her eyelashes at Ralph as she leaned over to take a hit.

"Okay, okay," Charlie said merrily, as he turned up the Bob Marley CD. "This trip is better than I thought it would be."

Ralph's hand reached up between the two front seats and waved the pipe gently back and forth.

"Not while I'm driving," Jen said. She was imagining Ralph's fingers on her thighs.

"Yes, yes, yes," Charlie said, reaching for the pipe and extending his other hand back for the lighter. "Wonderful. *Won-der-ful.*" He took several long, embarrassing hits and blew them out dramatically.

They were almost at the hot springs. Pamela was giggling in the back seat about something Ralph was murmuring. From the rearview mirror Jen saw that they seemed to be getting closer to each other, maybe even whispering in each other's ears? Charlie's head was plastered back against the seat rest. His eyes were closed, a big happy grin stretched across his mouth.

*Is this love, is this love, is this love, is this love that I'm feeling?*

"I have to pee," Jen said. "Badly."

"We need to get you stoned," Ralph said.

"I'm stoned," Pamela said, letting her head sink onto Ralph's shoulder. "What a blast."

Jen pulled a hard right into the hot springs turnout and everybody laughed gleefully as she slammed the brakes, hopped out of the minivan, and ran into the woods to pee.

**4**

"I'VE NEVER been here before," Ralph said as they started down the hill toward the hot springs. "Tell me when you want to get baked." They had to cross the river at the bottom of the hill and then hike up the other side. Charlie led the way.

Was Ralph impressed that Jen had been here before? Did he think she was a free spirit? The day was gorgeous: bright sun, cool breeze, clear sky. Yellow wild flowers on long stems leaned toward the dark wet ground. The damp soil squished beneath Jen's rubber sandals and wet her toes. She tried not to think about it, because what could she do, but in Albuquerque she missed water, she missed rain, dew, fog. She missed the ocean. In the summer, the Rio Grande became a muddy trickle, the public pool near their house was engulfed in a chlorine haze. The city was so dry it made Jen flat, dehydrated.

Jen saw Pamela slip her hand into Ralph's. The muscle in Ralph's arm shifted; he was squeezing her hand. Pamela was giggling hard. Why did she keep giggling? Did Ralph really know anything about Pamela? For example that Pamela gathered rainwater in barrels even though it almost never rained, that she bought local produce in season, period, or not at all? Did he know the real Pamela? Widow Pamela? Single mother Pamela whose two boys seemed to cry too easily and weren't great at T-ball? The Pamela who knew what "companion gardening" meant? This woman hanging onto Ralph's hand and laughing uncontrollably at nothing was not the real Pamela Hoffman.

"Who's going to jump in the river?" Charlie yelled. He dashed ahead, runner's muscles flexing under yellow nylon shorts. "Who's going do it?"

"I want to get baked," Jen said.

They let Charlie disappear downhill. Ralph took a quick look around then began his two handed maneuver holding the pipe and lighter.

"We'll catch him in a minute," Jen said. She inhaled.

A cloudy feeling immediately obscured her thinking. She inhaled again and again until Ralph said, "Whoa, lady, that's enough for now." Pamela seemed to look at her suspiciously, but maybe Jen was just paranoid from the pot. They started after Charlie, Jen behind Ralph behind Pamela.

"We have to find Charlie!" Pamela called out from the front of their line like an explorer. "Onward!"

Jen walked along behind Ralph and Pamela, feeling every bobble in her step, every root under foot, every rock, every splotch of mud giving way, and looking down, seeing every blade of grass, and looking up, seeing white clouds speed past.

Charlie was waiting for them at the bottom of the hill, on the close side of the small river that rushed fuller than Jen had ever seen it. He had his sweatshirt off already, his shoes and sneakers too. His face was just like their five-year-old son's when in a pique: determined, unyielding, foolish. Charlie looked thinner out here in the cool spring air than his body felt in her arms when she hugged him in the kitchen or held him in bed. He looked as though if he got in that river full of snowmelt he would crack his skull open and float away. Charlie threw his sweatshirt and sneakers to the other side of the river. It wasn't that wide, really, a series of six well-placed boulders to the other side.

"Charlie!" Jen yelled. "Charlie!"

"Watch this!" Charlie yelled. "It's gonna be spiritual!" He stood on alternating feet to take off his shorts and underwear and threw these across the river, where they landed next to his sneakers. He looked back at them once, his white butt rounder than Jen realized, then plunged into the water. Pamela screamed. Charlie fell over, howling, into the freezing water. Jen screamed, too. She hoped his howling and even falling were calculated beforehand, because usually she could count on Charlie to add effect upon effect. "Oh my God, Oh my God!" he was yelling, standing up, water flying from his body and sparkling through the air. Jen wondered if he had cut his bare feet, but then he was across and out of the river and racing up the hill.

Pamela and then Ralph and then Jen hopped the rock path across the river. Jen stopped to collect Charlie's scattered sneakers and socks, his shorts and underwear. Pamela and Ralph kept dashing along, Pamela like she was trying to keep up with Charlie, and Ralph trying to keep up with Pamela, both acting like they too were naked, soaked and frozen, desperate to get warm, but they weren't. No one had the balls to get into the river but her husband.

**5**

WHEN JEN REACHED the first pool of water, Pamela and Ralph and Charlie weren't there. A gang of what appeared to be high school kids in colorful bathing suits were hanging out in it, splashing and randomly hugging each other. Half-empty soda bottles and bags of chips ringed the pool in easy reach. A boy wearing Hawaiian-print board shorts stood under the warm waterfall that trickled; he laughed when he saw Jen holding sneakers and clothes. "Your man went that-away," he said in a friendly voice. Several of the girls wore frosty eye shadow and lipstick. They snickered. Jen gave them all a bland smile, decided she was too stoned to attempt a witty rejoinder, and walked a few steps toward the smaller pool.

Jen knew the smaller pool wasn't far; she could hear Pamela's voice ringing out. "Charlie!" But she couldn't hear the rest. Jen stood still for a moment between the two pools. Charlie and Ralph were in the hot spring with Pamela. How did that happen? It was supposed to be her in there with them. The aspen leaves were quaking; the sky was turquoise. How did anything happen? She remembered herself ten years ago, a bride, driving away from New York in a small rental car with Charlie, everything they owned, new towels, a cut glass decanter, locked in the trunk. As they drove through state after state, a lump lodged itself in her throat and a daydream, a hope, repeated its loop in her mind. Charlie would die when they got to New Mexico. It wouldn't be painful or sad. Somehow it would be quick. The marriage would be over: he would be dead and she would be free. She would rent the same car again and drive back to New York, to her real life, to herself.

"Charlie!" Pamela yelled again. Jen shook her head; Pamela sounded so pleased.

The path from the large pool to the small pool was well worn, through wildflowers and weeds. Pollen drifted through the air, making the daylight dreamy. There was Charlie in the small rocky pool, red-skinned, hair dripping, grinning triumphantly. Of course he was naked; she was holding his clothes. Pamela was naked, too, looking very happy, happier than Jen had ever seen her, actually, her usually severe face really shining with (drug induced?) happiness, and Ralph, also naked, sitting very close to Pamela. In fact, Ralph's arm was draped around Pamela's shoulder, his hand dangling alarmingly close to what must be her bare breast floating just beneath the water. He looked more satisfied than happy; what made him so smug? Pot did this to Jen, made her see so clearly. She couldn't have what she thought she wanted; it made her sad.

"Come in," Charlie said, holding out his hand. "Come here."

"We want you in here," Ralph said, looking up at Jen. She wouldn't try anymore to decipher his grins. She would try not to.

"Mmm, come on," Pamela said, smiling with her eyes closed. "Life is short."

Jen kicked off her rubber sandals, pulled her t-shirt

over her head, unsnapped her shorts and let them fall. She stepped out of the shorts and stood on the rocky rim of the hot spring in her bra and underwear. She was seriously stoned; she didn't care too much about her too curvy hips, didn't flinch at the shrill sound of a high school voice.

"Oh, God. They're all naked over there!" The voice floated over to the small pool from the big one: young, female, flabbergasted, disgusted.

Jen looked at Charlie, who was looking at her, and granted, he was stoned, too, but her husband was looking at her with more love than she could ever have imagined accruing or harvesting in her whole lifetime of ups and downs with him. And it wasn't over yet. She didn't deserve it, all his love. She took off her bra and underwear. Pam's eyes were still shut, but Charlie and Ralph looked at her body appreciatively. Another grin from Ralph. Charlie still held out his hand. The giggles she heard behind her from the big pool were a kind of old fashioned music, a dated soundtrack. She kept it behind her, that retro tune from another life, took Charlie's hand once again, and let him pull her into the hot water.

# ACKNOWLEDGMENTS

I am grateful to the writers who read versions of these stories: Veer Frost, Joan Dempsey, Dawna Kemper, Christa Mastroangelo, Nancy Zafris, Tara Ison, Frank Gaspar, and Kathleen Holt.

I am also grateful to the editors who published these stories originally.

Thank you Dan, Oliver, and Barry; I couldn't have written this book without you!

For love, encouragement, and inspiration, thank you Mom and Dad, Mike, Jennifer, Jessica, Matthew, Christopher, Jeannie, my in-laws, my brothers and sisters-in-law, and all my nieces and nephews.

Thank you Littleford-Foxes, the Dieners, and the Cartmells.

Love and gratitude to Elyssa, Jen, Heather, Jennifer, Christy, Amy, and Ellen.

To Dan DeWeese, editor and friend, many thanks.